JESSICA BECK
THE DONUT MYSTERIES, BOOK 41
# COUNTERFEIT CONFEC-TIONS

The First Time Ever Published!

The 41$^{st}$ Donut Mystery.

Jessica Beck is the *New York Times* Bestselling Author of the Donut Mysteries, the Cast Iron Cooking Mysteries, the Classic Diner Mysteries, and the Ghost Cat Cozy Mysteries.

WHEN SUZANNE, JAKE, Momma, and Phillip decide to buy an old house and fix it up, they soon discover that the neglected property is being used as a base for an illegal operation. The more they dig into the old house, the more they realize that there are more problems with the fixer-upper than just wiring and plumbing, and they must investigate the case or risk losing everything.

For P, my dearly beloved,
who shared the triumphs and tragedies of remodeling an older home
with me
and lived to tell about it, even managing to make it mostly fun along
the way.
Emphasis on "mostly"!

## Chapter 1

WHEN MY HUSBAND FIRST brought up his idea for what to do for the next phase of his life, I did my best to be enthusiastic, but it was hard for me to fake it. After all, at least as far as I was concerned, neither one of us knew anything about fixing up old houses and flipping them for a profit. I blamed his desire on too many Pollyanna television shows and internet channels giving him false confidence, but it had been so long since he'd had a real purpose in life—probably as far back as when he'd left the state police—that I couldn't bring myself to quash the idea. While it was true that as a teenager, he'd helped an uncle remodel houses two summers during his college breaks, I still had to wonder how much knowledge had really stuck. Besides, where would he even get the money to buy the cheapest run-down house in April Springs? We had some savings but not nearly enough, and I didn't make enough from my donut shop to cover the down payment for a scooter, let alone a house.

Then Momma and Phillip came on board, and suddenly we were off to the races. Jake had a purpose again, I had what amounted to a second job, and Momma and Phillip had a stake in something they were both interested in.

If I'd known that Jake's new path would lead us straight into intrigue, buried secrets, and even murder, I would have put my foot down right then and there, but hindsight is indeed twenty-twenty, so I said yes, and in the end, it nearly ended up killing us.

"Suzanne, check this out," Jake called out to me as he sat at our computer in the living room of our cottage. "You're not going to believe this."

I walked over and glanced at the screen. There I saw the ugliest, most run-down shack I'd ever seen in my life, online or in person. "That's actually for sale? Who in their right mind would be crazy enough to buy a place like that in such obvious poor condition?"

He blushed a little as I told him what I actually thought about the property, but I didn't put it together at that point. "It's got great potential," he answered with a shrug.

"For a bonfire, maybe," I said.

I still didn't get why he was persisting in defending the place, but he pushed on. "Look at the location. It's halfway between April Springs and Union Square, so it's off most people's radar. I drove out there this morning and took a look at it while you were at Donut Hearts. It's not as bad as it looks."

"It couldn't be, could it? Jake, why are you looking for another place to live? There's not something you're not telling me, is there?"

"Suzanne, I love living here with you. This cottage has always been a part of you, and now it's a part of me as well," he said. "This would be strictly for fun and profit."

"How could we possibly make any money off this wreck?" I asked. Okay, maybe I wasn't being as supportive as I always liked to believe that I was, but I still didn't have a clue where this conversation was going. Sometimes I can be as dense as the next person.

"Trust me, it's got good bones. Don't forget, I worked for Uncle Tim two summers in college doing exactly this." He must have noticed my budding frown, because he quickly continued, "I know how easy they make it look on television, but I've got the chops to do it. I built that closet, didn't I?" he asked as he pointed to the space under the stairs he'd converted into hidden storage.

"Yes, but you realize that an entire house is going to be a lot more work than that, don't you?"

"Of course I do, but we both know I need something to do with my time. I'm getting tired of freelancing as a hired hand on security details. This would give me a sense of purpose again, but if you're against it, I'll keep looking for something else."

The imploring look in my husband's eyes told me that he was dead serious about this proposal. I understood that Donut Hearts gave me a great sense of accomplishment, something that he'd been lacking in his life for some time, and he needed something that was just his.

I had to take this seriously.

"Okay, I understand completely, but where would we get the money for the materials you'd need to fix it up, let alone enough to buy it, even at that price? There's no bank in town that's going to loan us the money for that place."

Jake looked a little guilty about that, and I knew there was more to the story than I had heard so far. How long had he been planning this, anyway?

He looked a little guilty as he admitted, "Suzanne, there's something else I should tell you. I didn't go to the house alone."

"Okay," I said, trying not to overreact. "Who exactly went with you?"

"Well, the thing is, Phillip and I were going out to breakfast anyway, and he agreed to swing by and look at the property with me before we ate. It was all innocent enough."

I knew without asking that the Phillip he was referring to was my stepfather, a past nemesis of mine when he'd been our police chief who had gradually become a friend and ally as well as my mother's new husband. "I suppose he told you that he thought it would be fun, too."

"As a matter of fact, he said that he thought it would be the perfect thing to give him something to do, too. We'd do it together."

I knew that the men in my life had become friendly over time, but I'd had no idea they were close enough to go into business together. Besides, between the two of them, they still didn't have enough money to pull this off.

But I knew someone who did.

"Let me guess. Momma's going to finance the entire project." My mother was an extremely successful businesswoman, with assets spread throughout the South. Even I had no idea how much she was really worth, but I knew that she could afford this as a lark from her petty cash. "Has she even seen it?" It was my last hope, that my mother's business sense would outweigh any sentimentality for the two men closest to her.

"She might have dropped by while we were there," Jake admitted.

"Don't tell me. She already bought it, didn't she?" I asked, realizing that there was no way I was going to win this battle, so I might as well get on board.

"She put down a twenty-four-hour option on it," Jake replied. "I told her that there was no way I was going to do this without your full blessing. So what do you say?"

"Shouldn't I at least see it first for myself?" I asked.

"I'm not sure that would help convince you," Jake hedged. "Any chance you'll just trust us on this?"

"I suppose there's a little bit of one, but I want to speak with my mother first before I commit to anything."

Jake glanced at the clock. "That's convenient, because they'll be here in five minutes."

"Just how long have you been working on this?" I asked my husband, more out of curiosity than anything else.

That's when the doorbell rang. "Saved by the bell. They're early," Jake said. "What should I do?"

"You might as well let them in," I said, doing my best to smile, even though I felt a growing sense of dread. I had the distinct impression that this was a tidal wave I was too weak to fight alone.

My mother, ever petite and yet one of the most powerful people I knew, burst in before I could even say hello. "Suzanne, I know what you're thinking, but this truly is a great business opportunity. Don't say no until you've heard me out."

"Hi, Momma. How are you? It's a lovely day out, isn't it?"

She caught the forced sunshine in my voice and took a deep breath before replying. "You're right. I'm very sorry. Hello, sweetie. How are you?"

"Honestly, I'm a bit taken aback at the moment. It's kind of over-whelming to have three people I care so much about ganging up on me," I answered honestly.

At least Phillip had the sense to look embarrassed. "Hi, Suzanne."

"Hey, Phillip," I said before turning back to my mother. "Go on, Momma. I'm listening."

"The house is in a prime location, and it's got solid bones. I had one of my people go through it, and while it's true that it needs a great deal of work, it's all manageable. I'm positive that Jake and Phillip can handle anything that comes their way, but if they do happen to get in over their heads—which, as I said, I don't think will happen—I've got skilled craftsmen standing by to step in and lend a hand."

"Only if we ask for it, though," Jake said. "Remember, that was our agreement."

"Of course," Momma said. "Suzanne, it will be fun. Trust me."

I had to laugh. "Really? Fun? Okay, if you say so. You're all making it very hard for me to say no."

"Honestly, I think it sounds like a blast," Phillip said. I had a hunch he'd have agreed to hunt truffles if Jake were involved. My stepfather had the utmost respect for my husband, which I appreciated, but it could be a bit much at times. How he'd feel about him after working together on a dilapidated old house was another thing altogether, but at the moment, that wasn't my problem.

"We can do this, Suzanne," Jake added, looking as hopeful as a schoolboy.

"Let's say you go ahead with this," I said. "What happens when you sell this converted palace? I know you've come up with a financial scenario for an endgame, so don't try to pretend that you didn't."

"The men split all of the profits however they see fit," Momma replied.

"Fifty-fifty, right down the middle," Jake said, and Phillip happily nodded in agreement.

"I'm sorry, but that's not going to be good enough," I said.

"An equal split with Phillip is the only way I'll do it," Jake said, defending his potential partner.

Phillip looked a little hurt by my statement, so I knew that I had to fix it, and fast, especially since that wasn't what I'd meant at all.

"Hear me out. Momma, you're supplying the funding *and* the back-up expertise," I said. "You've never made a deal like this in your life, and I'm not about to stand idly by and let you do it now. You need to split the profits three ways. It's only right."

My mother wasn't ready to give in so easily. "No, that won't work, either. Now that you mention it, this needs to be a four-way split. We are going to form an LLC and do this right, and we're *all* going to have equal shares."

"Hang on a second," I said. "Don't go trying to drag *me* into this."

"Suzanne, can you honestly tell me that you won't be over there every spare minute you have?" Momma asked me. "Don't bother answering, we all know that it's true. You should have a share as well. It's going to be all for one and one for all. What do you say?"

I glanced at Jake and knew that I couldn't resist any further. After all, it was the best setup I could hope for, and with Momma's backing, both in money and in needed expertise, it was tough to say no. But even if none of that had been true, I knew that I was still going to agree after glancing at Jake's expression. He needed this nearly as much as I needed my donut shop. Whether I liked it or not, I was going to be in business with my husband, my mother, and my stepfather. "Okay, I'm in. Have the papers drawn up, and I'll give you my blessing." Maybe I'd get lucky and the deal would fall through. At the very least, I'd bought myself some time.

Or so I thought.

Momma reached into her oversized purse and pulled out what was clearly a set of contracts. I took one from her and scanned the pertinent information. "How did you know this was how we'd end up? This paperwork says we're forming a four-way partnership, but we just agreed to do it this way."

"What can I say? I had a feeling that was where we'd land in the end," Momma said, brushing my protest aside. "What do you say? Shall we move forward together?"

"Fine. SJDP Enterprises it is." It was our first initials, and I was flattered that Momma had put mine first. I knew how much she respected Jake and loved her husband, so it was quite an honor. "Thanks," I said as I handed the papers back to her after signing them all.

"Thank you. Suzanne, as you said earlier, I plan on making money on this arrangement, just like every other deal I've made in the past. I have a good feeling about our new venture."

Too bad she was wrong about that, but I couldn't really blame her.

After all, we were *all* starting out with high hopes.

We just didn't know how things would end up.

Which was probably a very good thing indeed.

"Wow, the pictures didn't lie, did they?" I asked the next day a little after noon as I got my first glimpse of the property my mother had just purchased for our joint venture. "It's quite a mess, isn't it?"

"You should have seen it before," Jake said with a happy grin as he started wolfing down one of the sandwiches I'd made for both men. They were filthy and obviously tired but just as apparently deliriously happy.

"You should see the dumpster," Phillip said as he paused between bites. "It's nearly full already."

"Are you two going to stop for the day, then?" I asked hopefully. While Jake wasn't exactly a young man, my stepfather was at least twenty years older than he was, and I worried about how much stamina he actually had.

"The plan is to work until three," Jake said, and I saw my stepfather flinch at the statement. My husband must have caught it as well. "Then again, I may be done for the day. I'm kind of beat. How about you, Phillip?"

"I'll do whatever you do," he said, though he was clearly happy with the reprieve. "But a hot bath and a nap might be nice, too."

They grinned at each other, and I was happy to see that at least so far, their partnership was holding strong.

"That sounds like a solid plan to me," I said.

"Knock, knock, neighbor," a portly older man said as he tapped on the doorframe. In one hand he had a six-pack of beer, and he smiled as he added, "Hope I'm not catching you at a bad time."

"Hey, Curtis," Jake said. "This is my wife, Suzanne."

"The donutmaker," the stranger said as he smiled at me. He noticed the bag of food in my hands. "Sorry. I didn't mean to interrupt. I just thought you could use a cold break."

"Thanks," Phillip said as he took the offering from him.

Curtis looked around and whistled. "I've got to tell you, I admire your ambition. I thought about buying this place and tackling it myself, but even at what it cost you, it was still more than I could scrape together. I'm looking forward to seeing your progress."

"We'll be here working on it every day," Jake said, and the man nodded and waved before disappearing.

"What was that all about?" I asked once the neighbor was gone.

"It appears we've acquired ourselves a spectator," Jake said. "I just hope he doesn't get to be a pain. The man's already popped in three times to check on our progress. I'm not sure what we're going to do with him."

"He'll get bored and find something else to do with his time," Phillip said. "I'm guessing he's harmless enough."

"If you say so," Jake said as he stared at the bag in my hand as he finished his sandwich. "Is there anything else in there for us?"

"Another sandwich apiece," I said as I handed the bag over. "What can I do?" I asked them.

"You brought food," Jake said. "That's a lot."

"Nonsense. If I'm going to be an equal partner, then I'm going to work, too." I'd made up my mind at the donut shop that morning that I was going to be more than just a secondary player in all of this. I was going to do my share of the hard labor as well. After all, in for a penny, in for a pound, as far as I was concerned.

"You don't have to do manual labor, Suzanne," Jake protested. "You've already put in a full day's work at Donut Hearts," he said as the men dug into the second set of sandwiches I'd made for them.

"I want to," I said. "After you eat, why don't you both go get some rest, and I'll work around here on the cleanup a little more?"

"Suzanne, I can't let you do that," Jake said.

I stared at him fixedly and just smiled without saying a word.

After a full twenty seconds, he relented. "You know what? On second thought, that would be great. Thanks."

I could see Phillip start to form a protest of his own, but Jake shook his head slightly, and my stepfather backed down immediately.

Once that was settled, I asked, "Where should I get started?"

"We haven't even touched the loft or the basement," Jake said. "If it's all the same to you, I'd rather you didn't go downstairs. I'm not sure about what we're dealing with there."

I didn't have to have my arm twisted. The truth was that I had no desire to go down where wild things might be, and it wouldn't have surprised me one bit if there had been whole communities of critters set up down there in the house's long absence of residents. "The loft it is," I said.

"If you open the window, you can chuck stuff out straight into the dumpster," Jake suggested.

"How much is up there?" I asked, wondering what I'd just gotten myself into.

"It appears that whoever had this place was a bit of a hoarder," Jake admitted, "but if you wear a mask and use some heavy gloves, you should be fine." After another bite of his sandwich, he asked, "Are you sure you don't want me to stick around? You probably shouldn't be here by yourself."

"She won't be," Momma said as she came in and joined us. She was wearing sturdy clothes, clearly ready to work, but she still managed to be stylish doing it, something I had not inherited from her.

I looked as though I'd outfitted myself at a yard sale.

"I've come to help as well."

"Dot, I thought we agreed. You're supplying the financing, and we're supplying the brute force," her husband said gently.

"Come now, Phillip, you don't honestly think I'd agree to that, do you? I haven't had a chance to work with my daughter for years. It will give us a chance to catch up."

At least he knew better than to argue with Momma about it, and we didn't hear a peep out of Jake. He too had learned the foolishness of going against my mother without having something dire at stake in the matter. After my husband finished his sandwich, he asked, "You didn't happen to bring any dessert with you, did you, Suzanne?"

"Just a couple of fritters left over from the shop," I said as I pulled out the last two things still in the massive bag I'd brought with me. "You don't have to eat them if you don't want to, though. They're probably stale anyway."

"I'll take my chances," he said as he eagerly reached for one of the wrapped fritters. Instead of eating it himself though, he offered it to his partner in renovation. "What do you say, Phillip?"

My stepfather glanced at my mother, who nodded her approval with a broad grin. "You've worked hard this morning. I'd say you've earned it."

"I agree," Phillip said with a grin as he eagerly pounced on the offering.

After they were finished eating dessert, the men took their leave, and Momma turned to me and smiled. "Thank you, Suzanne."

"For what?"

"For letting them do this," she replied. "It was important for both of them to feel useful again."

"I know," I said. "I'm surprised you're digging into the dirty work too, though."

"You shouldn't be," she said a little loftily. "You know as well as anyone that I'm not afraid to get my hands dirty."

"I have a hunch that it's going to be more than your hands, but I'm happy to have you here with me."

She hugged me briefly. "As am I. Now, what should we tackle first?"

I pointed to the stairs. At least they looked sound enough. "I've been told that our services are needed to clean out the loft."

"Then by all means, let's get to it," she said, pulling on a pair of heavy work gloves as she ascended the steps.

I had no choice but to follow. I wasn't exactly looking forward to going through someone else's trash and discards, but then again, at least I'd have my mother as company, and no matter what, she was a fun person to have by my side.

Chapter 2

"THIS IS REALLY QUITE a mess," Momma said as she threw the single window at the top of the loft open. "I wonder when someone was last up here."

"My guess is that it's been years, based on the amount of sheer junk that's here," I said. The smells on the first floor of the cottage had been muted when I'd come in, but up in the loft, we were getting the full force of an overwhelming combination of unpleasant odors. "Did something die up here or what?"

"Suzanne, bite your tongue," Momma said as she gingerly nudged with her foot the edge of a pile of old newspapers nearly three feet tall and almost eight feet long.

I didn't know if it was because of my past experience finding bodies or just my overactive imagination, but I could easily see how a corpse could be buried beneath the overflowing newspapers. "You *have* to smell it too," I said. "I wonder what the guys found downstairs this morning? I'm willing to bet it was nothing like this."

"Well, there's nothing we can do about it now except get to work removing it all," Momma said as she looked at the piles of debris with obvious discomfort. "There's no point in tarrying. Let's dig in."

"Why not?" I asked as I pulled my own gloves on. "What's that?" I asked her a moment later as I felt something just under the newspapers.

"Suzanne, if you are trying to frighten me, I don't appreciate it," my mother said sternly.

"I'm not kidding around, Momma." I reached deeper into the pile despite my better judgment telling me to run, not walk, downstairs and out of the house immediately. I pulled a few papers delicately aside to see what I could uncover without thrusting my entire hand into the pile.

An old can of processed meat had ripened over time and exposure and had exploded, filling the air with the ghastliest scent. "I may have found our problem," I said as I disposed of it out the window.

"At least one of them, at any rate," Momma said. "We've certainly tackled a big project, haven't we?"

"Are you talking about the loft or the house in general?" I asked as I started gathering up more newspapers and shoving them out the window as quickly as I could. Some of them started to blow away the moment they made it through the opening, and I was about to go downstairs after them when I noticed something particularly odd happening outside.

It wasn't just newspapers being caught by the wind and blowing around.

I also saw at least a dozen twenty-dollar bills wafting to the ground as well.

"It's raining money out there," I told my mother as I stood there, shaking my head in disbelief.

"Suzanne, you may as well stop, because you're not going to convince me to look out the window, no matter what."

I reached down into another pile of newspapers and found more money. As I held a few of the weathered but still nice twenty-dollar bills of the new design out to her, I asked, "How about this? Would you care to look at these?"

Momma was about to say something when she saw the money in my hand. "Where did you get that?" I could swear that her tone of voice was almost accusatory, as though I'd produced those bills myself just to get her attention.

"They were in that pile of newspapers," I told her as I handed them to her.

"Are they real?" she asked me.

"They look legit to me, but what do I know? I'm just a donutmaker," I said as I pulled my gloves off and grabbed my cell phone. "I hate to do it, but I'm going to get Jake over here right now."

"Phillip needs to hear about this as well," Momma said as she pulled off her gloves and made her own call.

As we waited for their return, we kept digging into the newspaper piles, but the rest of our efforts were in vain. We found a great deal of old newsprint, but no more money.

"Where is it?" the men both asked as they bounded up the stairs together. "Is it the same as this lot?"

Evidently they'd recovered some of the money I'd accidentally tossed out the window earlier.

"It has to be," I said as I handed Jake my batch while Momma gave her husband the rest of it.

"What do you think?" Phillip asked Jake with a frown after he examined a few bills in his hand.

"The same thing you do," my husband said.

"It just doesn't make any sense, does it?" Phillip asked him.

"Not yet," Jake replied.

"Would you two Sherlocks care to share what you're thinking with us mere mortals?" I asked them plaintively. "After all, we're the ones who found the stash. Don't worry, we'll split the reward with you. Maybe not fifty-fifty, though," I added with a grin.

Momma shook her head. "No, Suzanne, don't even tease about that. The four of us are in this together. Whatever we get for finding this, we split it four ways."

"I was just teasing," I told Momma. "They know that."

"It's a moot point, anyway," Jake said with a frown.

"It's not counterfeit, is it?" I asked him. I couldn't believe I hadn't thought to hold them up to the light to check for the security strips and holograms, but then again, I hadn't been expecting to stumble across a handful of fake money. The bills had looked real enough to me, but as I'd told Momma, it wasn't exactly my specialty.

"They are good ones, there's no doubt about that, but they are fake just the same," Jake said. "Do you agree?"

"I do," Phillip said.

"Whoever made them must have dyed them in tea and laid them out between the newspapers to age a little," Jake said. "I'm guessing that whoever manufactured them didn't know this house was going up for sale so quickly. The counterfeiters are going to be surprised when they come by and find that the locks have been changed and the loft has been cleaned out."

"Do you have any contacts you can call at the Secret Service?" Phillip asked Jake.

"Why the Secret Service and not the Treasury Department, or even the state police?" Momma asked the two former law enforcement officers.

"Counterfeiting is under the purview of the Secret Service, and they've been under the Department of Homeland Security for quite a while," Jake answered. "As a matter of fact, the Secret Service has been handling counterfeiting longer than they've been charged with protecting the president. Fortunately, I happen to know an agent I can call."

It didn't surprise me. My husband had been a member of the North Carolina State Police for so long that he'd developed relationships with all sorts of other law enforcement officers. "Is it anyone I know?" I asked him, since I'd met more than a few over the years since we'd been together.

"No, I met Agent Blaze long before we met," he admitted.

"Is that really his name? Blaze? That's so cool," I said.

"Actually, he's a she. Her name is Courtney Blaze, actually," he said almost apologetically. "She's very good at what she does."

"I just bet she is," I said, trying to keep my voice calm and level. There wasn't any doubt in my mind that my husband loved me dearly, but I also knew that he was an attractive man who had been very good at his job, something that tended to get competent women around him interested.

"Suzanne, we had a professional relationship only," Jake explained before he dialed her number.

"I don't doubt it for a second," I said, and almost as an afterthought, I kissed his cheek lightly. "Go on. Make that call."

Jake nodded, and I noticed that as he dialed a number in his phone, Momma looked on with approval. I loved it when she witnessed me being a grownup about something. Even at my age, my mother's blessing was very important to me.

Jake stepped to one side and lowered his voice as he had the conversation, and as he did, I started to bend down to look for more treasure we might have missed.

Phillip touched my shoulder lightly. "Suzanne, I wouldn't do that if I were you. We need to let the authorities finish the investigation."

"Momma and I have been sorting through these newspapers since we first found the bills," I said.

"I know that, but I've had a few brushes with the Secret Service in the past myself, and it's been my experience that they don't like anyone anywhere near one of their cases."

"Okay. I don't really need a reason not to work, anyway," I said with a grin to show that there were no hard feelings.

Momma approached me as Jake continued to speak on the phone with his contact. "Suzanne, you're handling this all rather well. It's good to see that you realize there's nothing for you to be jealous about."

"I know that better than you do," I told her with a smile. "I trust my husband with all my heart."

"This time it's trust placed wisely," Momma said, no doubt referring to the fact that my first husband, Max the Great Impersonator, had cheated on me while we'd been together.

"Who do you think is behind this?" I asked her softly, wanting badly to change the subject.

"It might be someone from Union Square *or* April Springs," Momma replied.

"Not a stranger to the area?" I asked her, curious about her reasoning.

"No, I doubt a stranger would just leave counterfeit money lying around. Whoever did this was obviously familiar with this house."

"Not enough to realize that it had been sold, though," I said.

"That's clearly true," Momma said as Jake got off his call and dialed another number immediately.

"What did she say?" I asked him.

"One second," he replied as he held up one finger in my direction. When the call went through, he said, "Chief, it's Jake Bishop. We've got a situation out at the house we're flipping. No, no dead bodies this time. Counterfeit money. I already called them. They are on their way, but they want some of your men here pronto to guard the place until they get here. No, I was told specifically to contact you directly. I know, but what can you do but comply with the request? We're not going anywhere, but if I were you, I'd hurry on over here myself. See you soon."

After Jake hung up, he said, "Sorry about that. Blaze is on her way, but she wants local law enforcement to guard the site until she gets here. She's close to an hour away, and I told her I'd hang around until she got here. Is that okay with you?" he asked me.

"We'll all stay, if that's an option," I said. "At least I will," I added, realizing that I'd just spoken for Momma and Phillip without asking them. "You two can take off if you want to."

"Are you kidding? I'm not going anywhere," Phillip said eagerly.

"Nor am I," Momma added.

"Then let's go outside and wait for Chief Grant to show up," Jake said.

"Is that really necessary?" I asked him.

"Trust me, you don't want to be in the house when Blaze gets here," Jake said knowingly.

I knew better than to question my husband's judgment about something I didn't know anything about. "Then let's go outside. I wonder if we missed any other bills during our search?" I asked as I glanced at the pile of papers still there.

"If you did, you'd better believe that they'll find them," Jake assured me. "Let's go, folks."

We made it outside ten full minutes before the April Springs police chief showed up on the scene along with two of his deputies. "The scene is secure," Jake told him.

"Are you hanging around?" Stephen Grant asked, clearly a bit nervous about dealing with the Secret Service by himself.

"If you don't mind," Jake said, not mentioning that he had been requested to be there when his contact arrived.

"Are you kidding? I'd love it," Chief Grant said.

"What's up, neighbor?" Curtis asked as he joined us. It was pretty obvious that he'd noticed the police cruisers whizzing past his house on their way to us.

Jake took one look at him and shook his head. "This isn't a good time, Curtis. You need to head back home."

"Got it. Just checking up on you," the man said with a nod, and then he vanished down the road to head home again.

Reinforcements came in less than half the time they'd promised.

Evidently the Secret Service was in a hurry to get started.

Chapter 3

"IT'S BEEN A LONG TIME, Bishop," the beautiful redhead in a tailored black suit said as she approached my husband and offered her hand. It appeared that she'd really wanted to hug him instead, but I wasn't sure if it was because of my presence or the agents under her on her heels, but she changed her mind at the last second. This woman was not only lovely, but she was also clearly self-assured. The two agents with her stood a few steps away with their hands folded behind their backs, and it was clear from the start that she was the agent in charge of this particular operation.

Jake smiled gently. "Hello, Blaze. Thanks for coming."

"Happy to. After all, it's part of the job," she said, her smile quickly fading. "Now, tell me what happened here."

"My wife and her mother were helping my father-in-law and me clean out this house we're flipping when Suzanne found the first few bills." He turned to me. "Suzanne, this is Courtney Blaze. Blaze, this is my wife and her mother, Dorothea. That's her husband, Phillip."

"Is that what you're doing now, working *construction*?" she asked, clearly not approving of my husband's new choice of careers.

"What can I say? It sounded like fun," Jake explained.

"Okay, I can see that," Blaze said. She ignored the others for a moment as she shook my hand and looked me straight in the eye for an instant longer than was entirely necessary. After a moment, she asked me quizzically, "Do I smell donuts?"

"That's me. I came here straight from the donut shop," I explained. I'd honestly stopped noticing the scent of freshly fried donuts that constantly hovered around me a long time ago, but I knew it could be a powerful aroma that clung to my clothes and my hair until both had a thorough wash.

"You work in a donut shop," she said with a hint of a frown as she nodded before releasing my hand.

"She does more than that; she owns the place. It's called Donut Hearts," Jake explained. It was clear that he'd caught the edge in her voice, and the change in her expression as well. "The place is extremely successful."

"Well, I wouldn't go that far," I said, happy that my husband had come to my defense. Then again, I was a grown woman, so I could take care of myself. "I manage to do all right for myself."

She accepted that, briefly nodded to Momma and Phillip, and then turned back to my husband. "Where are the bills you found?" she asked.

Jake produced everything that we'd found, all neatly bundled in a clear plastic evidence bag. It wasn't that unusual for him to carry the bags with him, since my husband had a pile of them on hand ever since he'd left the force. He'd even taken the time and trouble to fill out the information openings on the front, including the time, date, and contents of the bag.

Agent Blaze took the bag from him and nodded. "You always were an excellent law enforcement officer. I was surprised to hear that you left the force to get married."

"That wasn't the only reason, or even in the right order," Jake explained. "It was time. I needed a change in my life."

"And yet you've still managed to do some freelance work in security lately," Blaze said matter-of-factly.

"Keeping tabs on me, Blaze?" Jake asked her with a slight smile.

"I hear things from time to time." After offering him a brief grin, she was all business again, switching her personality off and on like a light. "Hang around for a bit, would you?" Blaze was most likely speaking to all of us, but you wouldn't know it, since she clearly had eyes only for my husband.

"We'd be happy to help in whatever way we can," I said with my brightest fake smile. It wasn't that I didn't like the woman. The truth was that she intimidated me. I'd always felt that way around redheads, especially striking ones, and this one exuded an air of confidence that was palpable.

"Good," she said as she turned toward Chief Grant. "Thanks for securing the scene. You're free to go."

"I thought I might stick around, too," the chief said.

"As long as you understand that you have no jurisdiction in this case. We're officially taking over," she said firmly.

"I get it," Chief Grant said simply.

"Perfect." She turned to her two agents. "Let's go."

They disappeared inside, and I noticed that she locked the door behind her, as though we might try to sneak in behind them to see what they might find. Okay, if I'd been alone I might have been tempted, but I thought it was a little excessive, given the circumstances.

Chief Grant whistled softly under his breath once they were gone. "I'm guessing you two have a history," he told Jake. It was a question I was dying to know the answer to as well, but there was no way I was going to be the one to ask him about her.

"We worked a few cases together back in the day," he admitted.

"Nothing more than that?" the chief asked.

"No. We were cordial, but that was it," he said.

"Okay," the chief said, dismissing that line of questioning. "Exactly how much money did you find up there?"

"Three hundred eighty dollars," Jake and Phillip said in nearly perfect unison. Both men nodded toward each other and smiled slightly.

I frowned. "I don't think they're going to find any more of those phony bills up in the loft. Momma and I looked pretty closely once we found the first few bills."

"Why the scowl?" Momma asked me, noticing my displeasure.

"Think about it. Would you go to all the trouble whoever printed those bills seemed to go to for less than four hundred bucks? You know, it's just as easy to counterfeit a hundred-dollar bill as it is a twenty. Why didn't they go for a bigger score, both in the worth of the bills they made and the sheer volume of their operation?"

"Hundreds are put under more scrutiny," Jake pointed out.

"Still, it seems like it's hardly worth the trouble. They clearly put a lot of time and energy into making those bills and then attempting to age them. I can't imagine this is the only stash of them they had, can you?"

"No, unless I miss my guess, I'd say this area is about to be flooded with bad paper," Jake said. "You might want to get a marking pen to make sure you're not getting any of the counterfeit bills."

"I've already got one," I said. I'd been burned a few months before with a bad twenty, and ever since, I checked them all. The new ones had watermarks and embedded plastic strips, but the old ones could be hard to spot by eye alone.

"Then you should be fine," Jake said. He pulled me aside and added in a lower voice, "Listen, I hope you know that there was never anything between me and Blaze."

"I wouldn't hesitate believing that for a second, but even you have to admit that she lit up the moment she saw you, and I doubt that's all that new."

Jake looked decidedly uncomfortable about the statement. "I never went out with her, Suzanne."

I took a leap and asked, "But she asked you out, or at least let you know that she'd be willing to date you if you were up for it, didn't she?"

"I can't do anything about that," Jake said stubbornly. "The point is that I never pursued her, not once."

I patted my husband's cheek and gave him a quick kiss. As I did so, I happened to glance up and found Agent Blaze watching us from the loft window above. She blushed a bit when she realized that she'd been spotted, and I doubt that happened very often. Being a redhead, she turned a delightful shade of pink before looking away.

"I'm not worried," I said. "You're stuck with me, and I'm stuck with you."

"Wow, you make it all sound so romantic," Jake replied with a slight smile, and then, to my surprise, he kissed me soundly in front of Momma, Phillip, and the chief of police.

It was my turn to blush now.

Momma and Phillip pretended to ignore us, but I noticed that Chief Grant was grinning broadly in our direction.

It was over half an hour before we saw any more movement from inside the house, and the chief kept glancing at his watch the entire time. "How much longer do you think they'll be in there, Jake?"

"It's hard to say. Blaze is thorough, so it will take as long as it takes."

"Well, I can hang around a few more minutes, but then we have to get back to work." I noticed his deputies were sitting in the car again, waiting patiently for their boss, but then why shouldn't they be happy enough to sit, since they were clearly still on the clock?

As Chief Grant spoke, I saw all three Secret Service agents approach the front door. Once they were outside, Blaze said, "We're going to have to secure the scene for the time being."

"Did you find any more bills inside?" Jake asked her.

She wanted to tell him, I could see it in her eyes, and if he'd been alone, there was no doubt in my mind that she would have told him everything, but clearly our presence kept her from saying too much. "Sorry, we can't disclose that at this time."

"When can we get the house back?" Phillip asked.

"We should be ready to release it by tomorrow morning. Was anyone on site besides the four of you?"

"Not today," I told her.

"A neighbor down the road stopped by a few times. His name is Curtis Mason, and he lives right over there," Jake said as he gestured to the neighbor's home.

She nodded. "Understood. Jake, your prints are on file. How about the rest of you?"

"I used to be the chief of police in April Springs, too," Phillip said.

"I've supplied mine to local investigations in the past," I admitted.

That caught her attention. "Were you a detective as well in a previous life?"

"Not in any official capacity," I admitted.

She waited for me to explain further, but I decided to follow my husband's example and keep my answers short and to the point.

"And you?" she asked Momma.

"No, not that I'm aware of," she admitted. "Is that really necessary? I wore gloves the entire time I was inside."

"If you don't mind, it will aid us in our investigation if we can eliminate as many sets of fingerprints as we can," Agent Blaze said. It was clear that Momma avoiding being fingerprinted wasn't going to be an option.

"You can use my equipment in April Springs if you'd like," Chief Grant offered.

"Thank you, but that won't be necessary. We have a kit in the car."

Momma followed one of the agents to get fingerprinted, with Phillip close on her heels.

"Do you need me to keep the place under surveillance?" the chief asked her.

"Thank you, but as I said, we've got the scene covered. Thank you for your cooperation."

It was a dismissive tone, and there was no mistaking it. The chief just nodded and then tipped his cap to us. "In that case, I'd better be getting back. See you two later."

Once he was gone, it was just the three of us, since the remaining agent had stationed himself in front of the door and had taken himself out of the equation.

Jake pulled out a key on a string that had a tag with the house address on it. "You'll need this. We just changed the locks this morning."

"Fine," she said. It was clear that Blaze wanted to say more, but I was obviously cramping her style.

That was fine by me.

"I'll touch base later," Blaze said.

"Do you need my address in April Springs?" Jake asked her.

"No, I've already got it," she replied before turning to me. "It was nice meeting you, Susan."

"It's Suzanne," I corrected her. "Likewise." I put my arm in Jake's and started to lead him away. "Let's go home, shall we?"

"I've got my truck, and your Jeep is sitting right beside it," Jake answered logically. "We can't really go together, can we?"

It ruined a perfect exit, but he was right. We'd both need our own vehicles once we were home. I resisted the urge to kiss him again in front of Agent Blaze. Instead, I said, "Sounds good. I'll see you back at the cottage."

"I'll be there," he said with a soft smile.

As I got into my Jeep and headed home, there were a few questions swirling through my mind. Who had been using our new project as a clearinghouse for counterfeit twenties? Was it indeed someone local, as Momma had suggested, or was it someone who had spotted what seemed like a deserted house and had taken advantage of it? Surely they'd try to come back to collect the efforts from their work, but would they spot the agents there before it was too late? Last but certainly not least, was my curiosity about just how long Agent Blaze was going to be in town and in our lives.

For everyone's sake, but mine in particular, I hoped it wouldn't be long, but I wasn't counting on it.

In the meantime, we needed to get life back to normal. I wasn't sure how long they'd keep the house for their investigation and observation, but one thing was certain.

No one would be working on fixing the place up again anytime soon.

Chapter 4

BEFORE I EVEN MADE it into the cottage, my phone rang. "Suzanne, do you and Jake have dinner plans tonight? I made a pot roast that's certainly large enough for the four of us, if you're interested," Momma said.

"Why on earth would you make something that big for just the two of you?" I asked her as I sat on the porch swing out front.

"I often make large meals and freeze most of it. I'm not sure why some people have such an aversion to leftovers. Phillip often likes them better the second time around, so we always have plenty on hand. What do you say? Or do you need to speak with Jake first?"

"No, I'm positive he'll agree to eat just about *anything* you make. You don't happen to have any pie too, do you?" I asked her.

"No. I'm sorry. I made a pineapple upside-down cake this morning, though. Would that do?"

"It would be perfect. Are you sure we're not putting you out?" I asked her as Jake drove up in his truck.

"We'd love to have you. Besides, it will give us a chance to discuss what happened earlier at the house."

"What time should we get there? You know I have to eat earlier than most people because of my work hours."

"I'm well aware of it, Suzanne. Is five too soon, or is that perhaps too late?"

"It's perfect. We'll be there. Thanks, Momma."

"It is always a pleasure to take care of my little girl," my mother said before hanging up. We both knew full well that I hadn't been a little girl in a very long time, but if it made my mother happy thinking of me that way, I wasn't about to argue with her.

Especially when there was good food and a dessert to boot waiting for me at her home.

"Good news. Momma invited us to dinner," I told Jake as he joined me on the front porch.

"And you accepted without even asking me first?" he asked me with a touch of frost in his voice.

"I honestly didn't think you'd mind. I can always call her back and cancel," I said, a little concerned that I'd misread my husband so completely.

Jake couldn't keep his stony expression a second longer. "Don't you dare," he said as he broke out in a grin. "It sounds great to me."

"Just for that, you're not getting any dessert," I said as I unlocked the door and let us both inside.

"Come on, I was just teasing. She made pie, didn't she?"

"As a matter of fact, she made a pineapple upside-down cake," I said.

"I love that, too," Jake said. After a moment's pause, he asked, "If I let you take your shower first and use all of the hot water, can I get back on the full menu plan, dessert included?"

I pretended to consider it for a few seconds before finally nodding. "I suppose that's a fair trade," I said as I raced for our bathroom. There was a shower upstairs I had used when I lived there with Momma, but the water pressure was much better in our bathroom suite. Besides, it was closer to the hot water tank, too, a key factor in getting quick delivery. I took a brief shower to spare him some hot water, and as he showered, I got dressed in fresh jeans and a T-shirt. Soon enough, we were on our way to Momma's place. I wasn't sure about Jake, but I was starving just knowing what was waiting for us there.

"Dot, you've outdone yourself yet again," Jake said as he pushed his dessert plate away. "Suzanne threatened to keep me from your cake, but I'm glad she didn't mean it."

"Suzanne Hart, why on earth would you do something so cruel?" Momma asked me with a twinkle in her eye.

"I had my reasons," I told her. The truth wasn't much, but the innuendo was perfect. Let her and Phillip come up with their own reasons in their minds. "It really was wonderful. All of it." I stood and started gathering plates, and to my happy surprise, Momma didn't say a word as I started to clean up. Usually she insisted on doing it herself. Maybe she was finally beginning to accept me as an adult and a friend, not just a daughter.

"Don't forget to rinse them before you put them in the dishwasher," Momma reminded me.

"I never do," I said, reverting to a younger tone I'd used in my teens.

"Rinse or forget?" Jake asked.

"Do you really want to get into the middle of this?" I asked him pointedly.

"No, ma'am. No thank you. Phillip, I'd love to talk to you about our plans for that master bathroom at the house."

It was an obvious dodge to extricate himself, but I didn't blame him. This was between Momma and me. Phillip picked right up on it. "Let's head off to the living room after we help finish clearing the table."

"You boys go," Momma said. "We'll handle it."

He paused long enough to kiss my mother's cheek. "Thank you, my dear. Have I told you lately that you're the best?"

"Yes, but I never tire of hearing it," Momma said, softening for a moment.

"Then I'll keep telling you until my dying breath," Phillip responded.

"Which we will both hope is a very long time away," Momma answered.

Once they were gone, I turned to my mother. "I'm sorry."

"About what in particular?" she asked me.

"For sassing you," I explained.

"Apology accepted." Momma studied the remains of dessert for a moment and shook her head. "There's barely enough left here to save."

"If you throw that out, Jake will shoot us both, if Phillip doesn't do it first," I told her.

"I wouldn't dream of discarding it," Momma said. In a softer voice, she said, "I've got two clean forks in the kitchen. Care to polish it off with me?"

It was the best peace offering I'd ever gotten in my life. "Lead the way!"

As we sat in the kitchen enjoying the cake straight from the serving platter, I asked her, "What do you honestly think about what we found at the house today?"

"Truthfully, I don't know what to think," Momma said. "It all seems a little too deliberate to be random, doesn't it?"

"What do you mean?"

"Suzanne, that house has been empty for years," Momma said. "Whoever is counterfeiting money there had to know that. Why else choose it as a spot to treat and dry their illegal currency?"

"That's what I don't get," I said. "Why not do it on their own kitchen table, or even in their basement or shed? Why risk losing it at a place they can't control?"

"It probably didn't seem all that risky when they chose the house in the first place. How could they know it was going on the market so quickly? Besides, what if they'd been caught red-handed with those bills? By processing them at the house, they were distancing themselves from their illegal activities."

"I suppose it makes sense when you look at it that way," I said.

I was about to add something more when I heard footsteps approach the kitchen from the living room. There was just one bite left of the dessert, and I made an executive decision and forked it into my mouth before there could be any formal protest.

"We were wondering if there was any of that pineapple upside-down cake left," Phillip said as he walked in with Jake close on his heels.

I was in no position to answer since my mouth was full of the remnants of our dessert, but Momma came to my rescue. "Sorry, but I'm afraid that it's all gone."

The look of disappointment on the men's faces would have been hilarious if it hadn't been so heartbreaking. Momma added, "There are some odds and ends of pies in the refrigerator, if you two are honestly still hungry. I'm sorry I can't offer you more than that."

Jake piped up immediately, though Phillip seemed a little reticent to accept her offer. "That sounds great," my husband said.

"Jake, do you honestly need *another* dessert?" I asked him, feeling a slight bit guilty since I'd just stuffed some down my own throat minutes earlier.

"Define need. I worked hard today, Suzanne. Don't I deserve a little extra?"

"Of course you do," I said, laughing at his pitiful expression.

"Why don't you two go back into the living room? We'll make some fresh coffee and bring that and the pie slices right out," Momma suggested.

"That sounds amazing," Jake said.

"Phillip, I noticed earlier you appeared to be hesitant about taking me up on my offer. Should I take that to mean that you don't want any more dessert yourself?"

"I don't know what you're talking about, my dear," he said with a grin. "I'm not sure how you got that impression, but if you're offering treats, I'm accepting. You don't even have to ask."

She laughed at her husband as well.

Once the men were gone, I said, "I'll gather up the rest of the dishes while you make the coffee and get the pie slices out of the fridge."

"Are you having some, too?" she asked me.

I was stuffed, but I wasn't about to admit it. After all, I was at least as big a fan of my mother's pies as my husband was. "Maybe a sliver or two," I said. "How about you?"

"I doubt I could hold one more bite, but you should feel free to have some if you'd like."

"I will, then."

Once we were all settled in the living room, our pie gone but some of the coffee still remaining, Momma asked, "How long do you think it will be before we get the house back, Phillip?"

Her husband shook his head. "I have no idea. That's way over my pay grade. Jake, you've dealt with the Secret Service before. What do you think?"

"I'm guessing it will be a minimum of three days, and the maximum could go on for months."

"That long?" I asked.

"The Secret Service takes their responsibilities very seriously," Jake said. "They won't just let it go. They can't afford to. Counterfeit money is bad for everyone involved."

"Except the crook who passes it off as being the real deal," I said. "How do they keep from getting caught, even once they make the phony money?"

"Mostly they're arrested after the first few tries, but sometimes they're cagey about it. I suppose it all depends on who's behind this scheme."

It was something to think about. "And in the meantime, Momma is losing money on her investment every day."

"Don't worry about that," my mother said as she waved a hand in the air. "That house is in a valuable area. I have great hopes that eventually Union Square and April Springs will grow into one large city."

"How long do you think that will take?" I asked her incredulously.

"Oh, most likely not in my lifetime, and perhaps not even in yours, but you have to keep an eye on the future."

"Thanks, but I think I'll stick to my daily speculation about how many donuts to make each morning," I told her. "That's enough of a peek into the future for me."

"Suzanne, sometimes you lack true vision," Momma said.

"I've never denied it," I said with a grin. "So, the project is on hold indefinitely. What are you two going to do in the meantime?"

Jake glanced at Phillip, who nodded in agreement. After getting approval, my husband said, "We were just discussing that in the living room. As a matter of fact, we were thinking about trying to catch the counterfeiter ourselves."

"What do you think Agent Blaze is going to say about that?" I asked him.

"Suzanne, you know better than most that sometimes the wheels of justice are slow, and I don't want to wait around forever to finish this house. Besides, what she doesn't know won't hurt her." He said the last bit with a grin.

Just then his cell phone rang. "Speak of the devil," he said as he looked at the caller ID. "I've got to take this." He stepped toward the front door.

"You don't have to go outside," I said.

"I won't be a minute," he answered as he hurried out the door.

Once he was gone, Momma asked, "What do you think that's about?"

"I wouldn't even care to guess," I said.

"She's rather attractive, isn't she?" Momma asked guardedly.

I thought she was talking to me, but for some reason Phillip decided to answer her. "I suppose some people might think so. As for me, I've never cared for redheads myself."

Momma looked at him and smiled. "Phillip, you'd have to be blind not to see that woman is beautiful, no matter what color her hair might be. It's fine with me if you admit it."

"Okay, she's drop-dead gorgeous," he answered a little too enthusiastically and a little too quickly.

"Let's not get carried away, though, shall we?" Momma asked him.

"No, of course not. Fine. She's a bit above average, truth be told, but not more than a little bit."

"You, sir, are a big fat liar," Momma said with a bright smile.

Phillip just shrugged, but I saw him hiding a smile as well.

Jake came back in a few minutes later. "Well, that's off the table."

"What is?" I asked him.

"Agent Blaze called to tell me to keep my nose out of her case and for the rest of you to do the same as well. She made it crystal clear that she doesn't want anyone muddying the waters, including me." He seemed hurt by the exclusion, but he'd better get used to it, since he didn't have any official standing anymore.

"It's okay. There are other things we can do in the meantime," I said as I patted his shoulder.

"Like what?" he asked.

"While I'm making donuts and Momma continues to run the world, you two can start gathering materials you'll need, design the kitchen and bathrooms, pick out light fixtures, and figure out a thousand other things you're going to be doing in the months ahead."

"Sure, that makes sense," Jake agreed reluctantly, "but I was really looking forward to doing a bit of detecting if I couldn't jump right into demolition work."

Phillip nodded in agreement. "There's nothing quite like knocking out a wall or two."

I had to laugh. "Don't worry, all of that will still be waiting for you once Agent Blaze releases the house to us again. In the meantime, start planning so you can hit the ground running when she finally releases the place back to us."

"Jake, was there *any* wiggle room at all in what she told you on the phone about us looking into this?" Phillip asked him tentatively.

"Trust me, we don't want to cross Blaze," he said. "She has a bite that's worse than her bark, and I've seen her reduce thugs to whimpering little schoolkids with her words alone. We need to drop this right here and now."

"Understood," my stepfather said with a grim nod of his head. "Do you still want to meet in the morning?"

"You heard Suzanne. We have a ton of planning to do. Let's grab a bite at the Boxcar, and then we can get started."

"Sounds good to me," Phillip said. For a change of pace, he was the first one to yawn, something that was usually reserved for me. "I don't know about you all, but I'm beat."

"I could sleep," Jake admitted.

"I can't believe that *I'm* not the one ending the party first," I crowed.

"Are you saying you're not tired, too?" Momma asked me.

"Oh, I'm wiped out. I'm just glad that I wasn't the first one to admit it." As we stood, I hugged Momma fiercely. "Thanks for tonight. It was wonderful."

"Your presence made it so," Momma said, squeezing me back just as tightly.

After we said our good-byes, Jake and I made our way back home. I thought about bringing Agent Blaze up again, but I decided to leave it, at least for now.

The less my husband thought about that intimidatingly attractive woman, the better, at least as far as I was concerned.

## Chapter 5

I WOKE UP AN UNTOLD amount of time later to the sound of voices in the living room. When I reached across the bed, I confirmed that Jake was gone. From what I was hearing, it was obvious that he wasn't alone, and I had a sneaking suspicion as to who he was talking to in the middle of the night. I stopped just long enough to grab a robe and some slippers and headed into the living room to see what was going on.

I found Jake sitting on the armchair and Agent Blaze perched on the edge of the sofa, apparently hanging on his every word. Or was that just my imagination?

"Suzanne, I'm sorry if we woke you," Jake said as he rose instantly and kissed me.

I noticed that Agent Blaze looked away for one second, and for some reason that made me smile. Could she actually be jealous of me? If she was, I was going to take comfort from that fact. "That's okay. Can I make you both some coffee?"

"No, I was just heading to the hotel, and I thought I'd stop by and give your husband an update," Blaze told me. "You have a lovely home." It was said almost automatically, but I happened to agree with her, so I just smiled.

"Thanks. What's going on? Or is there anything you can tell me?"

"I told Agent Blaze earlier that I would share anything she told me with you," Jake explained.

"And you're okay with that?" I asked her.

The Secret Service agent grinned for a moment, losing the severe look that seemed to be her natural expression. Wow, was I glad she didn't smile all of the time! She was way too stunning that way.

"Apparently I have to be. I just wanted to let you know that we're wrapping things up earlier than expected at the cottage."

"Really?" I asked as I sat on the sofa beside her. "I figured you'd be here for at least a few more days."

"The truth is that we caught a break," the agent said. "The counterfeiter came back to the house while we were still there. In a way, it was almost too easy."

"Who was it?" I asked her.

"A man named William Joseph Branch," she said. "His friends call him Slick Willie, and I can see why. Evidently word on the street is that he'll do anything for a buck. What can I say? Sometimes we get lucky."

"I've never heard of him," I said, "and I know just about everybody in April Springs."

"He's from Union Square, so that explains that. He waltzed right into the place as though he owned it, headed straight for the stairs, and we were waiting for him."

"Did he confess to counterfeiting those twenties?" I asked.

She shook her head. "No, but it's been my experience that criminals rarely confess, no matter what you might see on television or read in a book. Slick Willie denied everything. He claimed that somebody hired him through a third party. They gave him a hundred dollars to shine a light from the loft window, and that was all that he had to do. Once he accomplished that, he was promised two hundred more. I shouldn't be surprised. Willie's got a record a mile long. How ridiculous is that story?"

"Let me guess. The hundred you found on him was all in twenties, and they were all as fake as the ones we found earlier, and what's more, all of them were based on the new design of the twenties, not the old one," I said.

Agent Blaze looked at me with a new hint of respect. "That's exactly right. We've got him with his own bills in his pocket." She stood, and we followed suit. "Anyway, I just wanted to come by and let you know that you can have the house back." She turned to Jake. "It was good seeing you again, Jake," she said as she extended a hand.

He shook it briefly, and then Agent Blaze shook mine as well. "Mrs. Bishop, it was a pleasure to meet you."

I wasn't about to correct her. I really was Mrs. Bishop, though everyone in town still called me Hart. I had no intention of giving her any ideas that our relationship wasn't rock solid. "You, too. Feel free to stop by the donut shop in the morning on your way out of town, and I'll buy you a cup of coffee and a donut."

"Actually, I'll be here for the next few days," she explained. "I'm sorry, but I'm not allowed to accept gratuities, but I appreciate the offer."

"Happy to make it," I said.

After Agent Blaze was gone, I looked at Jake for a moment before I spoke. "Do you honestly believe that?"

"Believe what?" he asked, clearly preoccupied by something.

"That some small-time grifter was sophisticated enough to make those bills we found," I said.

"You heard what Blaze said. The man's a known con."

"Sure, but what I want to know is, has he ever been arrested for counterfeiting before?"

Jake kissed my nose. "You have a suspicious mind. You know that, don't you?"

"Hey, I thought that was why you loved me."

"Just one of many reasons," Jake said. "Anyway, all's well that ends well. We have the house back, and Phillip and I can get back to work in the morning."

"Don't forget, I'll be there after I close the donut shop," I promised him.

"Suzanne, I told you earlier today that you don't have to pull double duty every day. You know that, don't you?"

"What am I going to do without you? You've spent enough time away from me, sir. I plan to spend *all* of my free time off with you, no matter what you're doing. If that means cleaning out houses or mucking out stalls, then I'm in."

"If I know Agent Blaze, there won't be any more cleaning to do. I'm willing to bet that she's gone over every last inch of the place."

"I hope you're right," I said. "There's nothing like a clean slate to start with, is there?"

Jake laughed as he took my hand and led me into the bedroom. "That house is many things, but clean is not one of them."

"At least tomorrow we can get back to work," I said. "Are you going to call Phillip and tell him the good news?"

"I texted him the second I heard we were free to work again," Jake admitted. "We're still meeting bright and early tomorrow morning at the Boxcar Grill, and then we're going back to work on the house."

"I'm willing to bet that it won't be as early as I'm getting up."

"Suzanne, no one in their right mind would get up when you do by choice," he replied.

"Are you saying that I'm crazy?" I asked him with a grin.

"No more than usual, but I love you just the same."

"That's a good thing, because I doubt there's any hope for me changing."

"I'm counting on you staying just the way you are," he said with more than a hint of laughter in his voice.

The next morning, it was life as usual at Donut Hearts. It was almost easy to forget what had happened the day before at the flip house, though I still had my doubts that Slick Willie was the only culprit in the counterfeiting scheme. Then again, if it was good enough for Agent Blaze, then it needed to be good enough for me.

I had just finished dropping the cake donuts when Emma came in. "Have you gotten used to the new dropper yet?" she asked. Our original dropper had been used in a homicide on the premises, and we'd had to scramble to find a replacement. I'd pulled one of the antique ones from the wall, and after giving it a thorough scrubbing, I'd put it into immediate service.

"To be honest with you, I haven't even thought about it in weeks, so the answer is probably yes. How about you?"

"I love it. It's not nearly as heavy as the last one was, so I don't feel as though I'm taking my life in my hands every time you use it." She touched the spot on the wall where the old dropper had slipped out of my hands, and I had to smile.

"What fun is that?"

As she took off her light jacket and put on her apron, she grinned at me. "Making donuts shouldn't be a hazardous profession, Suzanne."

"Neither should flipping houses, but you never know," I said as I started on my yeast dough while Emma dove into the dishes.

"I heard about what happened at the place you're working on," Emma said.

"Let me guess. Your dad told you, right?"

"Hey, you can't blame him if he's hunting for news." She looked a little uncomfortable as she said it, and I wondered what was really on her mind.

"Emma, is there something you're not telling me?" I asked her.

"No. Not really. It's more of a question, to tell the truth."

"What is it? It's not like you to beat around the bush. We've known each other long enough that you should know you can be direct with me. I certainly do the same thing with you."

"Dad was wondering if he could come by on our break and talk to you about what happened," she said, her words rushing out of her. "You can say no, but I promised him that I'd ask, so I've fulfilled my part of our bargain."

"Sure. Why not?" I asked. After all, the case was over and done with, at least as far as the authorities were concerned.

"Seriously? You don't mind?" she asked a bit incredulously.

I thought about it for a few moments, and then I nodded my confirmation. The case was officially closed, there was no murder involved, and for once I hadn't been dragged into holding my own investigation because of circumstances. If anything, I was just an innocent bystander.

Well, innocent enough, at any rate. "I don't mind, but I'm not sure what I can tell him," I confessed.

"Oh, don't worry about that. The fact that you're willing to do it in the first place means a lot to me and Mom." Emma's mother, Sharon, had become nearly as visible a presence at Donut Hearts as we were. After all, in my absence, she ran the front while Emma made the donuts, so I was happy I could please both of the women who made my work life so much easier.

"It's my pleasure," I said. I glanced at the clock and saw that we were very nearly due to take our break together. "Do you need to call him first and tell him the news?"

Emma failed to hide her slight blush. "Actually, all I have to do is flip the front light on. If he sees it, he'll know you agreed. If the place stays dark, he won't bother us."

"That's a nice system you've worked out there," I said. "Why don't you go ahead and turn the light on, then?"

"Thanks. I will," Emma said as she pulled her hands out of the soapy water. "I'll be right back."

As soon as she was gone, I began to wonder if I should open myself up to the newspaperman after all. Ray Blake and I had endured more than our share of disagreements in the past, though lately we'd been trying to play nice, given the fact that Emma and Sharon were both parts of our everyday lives. In the end, I realized that it just didn't matter that much to me. I'd help him now, and that would give me leverage to say no the next time, if I ever happened to investigate another murder, which I sincerely hoped never came up. I would be perfectly satisfied if I never saw or had to deal with another dead body again for the rest of my life.

Emma came back in a flash. "Let me know when you're ready."

The dough was still mixing on its first go-round, so I took a moment to clean up my workspace a bit before I turned the mixer off. Emma wasn't nearly as keen on cleaning as she went as I was, but it was the only way I seemed to be able to get anything done in my kitchen when I was in charge.

The timer finally went off, and after flipping the switch and removing the hook, I covered the bowl with plastic wrap and reset the timer. "Are you ready to head outside?"

"I'm right behind you," she said as she pulled the last clean bowl out of the suds, rinsed it off, and put it in the drying rack with all the others. Making donuts tended to generate a great many dirty pots and pans, especially when I was creating the cake donuts. I always made a large batch of basic batter, and then I divided it into smaller portions so I could create all of the individual flavors of cake donuts we were offering for the day. I wondered sometimes if my customers had any idea how much work went into making their favorite treats, but to be fair, I loved my Jeep, but I had no idea how long it had taken to make, nor did I even care. All that mattered to me was that it ran when I needed it to and didn't give me too many problems along the way.

Could we expect anything more from our delightful donuts?

Chapter 6

"THANKS FOR DOING THIS, Suzanne," Ray said the moment Emma and I stepped outside the shop. The mornings were definitely getting warmer, and soon we'd be in the full bloom of summer, where it was less than comfortable even at four o'clock in the morning.

"Would you like me to leave you two alone while you chat?" Emma asked us.

"You're fine right where you are," Ray told his daughter quickly.

"I was talking to Suzanne," she corrected him.

"Of course you were," he replied.

"It's fine," I said. "We won't be long. There's really not all that much to talk about."

"I beg to differ," Ray said as he brought out a small notebook and started flipping through page after page of his sloppy scribbling. "I've got at least an hour's worth of questions here."

"I'm not sure how that's going to work. We have ten minutes, and then Emma and I have to get back to work. I suggest you hit the highlights," I said.

"I'm not sure I can," Ray said in dismay.

"Dad, she's doing you a favor. Don't forget that," Emma reminded him.

"Of course." He studied his notes for another ten seconds before he got started in earnest. "Suzanne, how did you first discover that something illegal was going on in your home?"

Wow, was that a leading question. If the tone of his article was that biased, I was going to have to shut this interview down on the spot. "First of all, it wasn't at my home. It occurred at a house my family is renovating between April Springs and Union Square."

"That's what I meant," Ray corrected me, clearly unhappy with my response.

"That may be, but it's not what you said," I told him.

"Let me start again," he said after taking a deep breath. "How did you happen to discover the counterfeit money at the house you and your family are remodeling?"

It was clear that Ray was already composing his story in his mind, but I tried not to let that bother me. "Momma and I were cleaning out the loft yesterday afternoon after Jake and Phillip tackled the first floor. There were a ton of old newspapers up there, and as we were throwing a stack of them out the window into the dumpster below, I saw some twenties floating through the air. We kept digging and found quite a few more."

"Could you tell initially that they were fake?" he asked me.

"No, at least I couldn't, but as soon as Jake and Phillip got there, they knew almost immediately. Then again, both men were seasoned lawmen before they retired." I was paying my stepfather quite a compliment by linking what he'd done with my husband's career, but I didn't see the harm in it.

"What did your mother think of the discovery?"

"You'll have to ask her that yourself," I replied. There was no way I was going to speak for my mother in any way, shape, or form, especially when it would probably end up in the newspaper.

"Okay, next question. Exactly how much did you find?"

"I'm not sure, exactly," I said. That wasn't true; I knew because Jake and Phillip had told me. I just wasn't sure I wanted to share that bit of information with Ray Blake.

"Guess," Ray said, and then waited patiently for me to answer.

"It was somewhere in the neighborhood of four hundred dollars," I finally admitted. "That's all I'm willing to say."

"What were the denominations?"

"All of them were twenties," I answered.

Ray took a few notes, then he flipped to his next question. "What did you do after you discovered the money?"

"I told you that already. I called Jake, and Momma called Phillip."

"No, I mean after the four of you determined that the money was counterfeit," he said, pushing me on it just a bit.

"We called an old contact of Jake's at the Secret Service. They handle counterfeiting, just in case you weren't aware of it."

"Of course I am," Ray said absently as he took another note.

"Well, I didn't know that," Emma said. "That's interesting. You'd think it was part of the treasury or something."

"That's what I thought too. The Secret Service used to be under them, but they're under Homeland Security now."

"Suzanne, I already know all of that," Ray said impatiently.

"I didn't, though," Emma replied, frowning at her father. "Dad, how am I going to learn if I don't ask questions? Isn't that what you're always telling me?"

It was clear that was exactly something Ray had told his daughter a thousand times before in the past, but he didn't seem to like having his words thrown back at him, especially at the moment. "Are there any suspects?" he asked me, ignoring his daughter's query.

"You honestly don't know?" I asked, surprised.

"Know what?"

"They've already made an arrest."

Ray Blake nearly dropped his pen. "What? When did that happen?"

I suddenly realized that I might have just said too much. "I'm not at liberty to disclose that information," I said, echoing something my husband used to say concerning things he wasn't at liberty to talk about. "You'll have to get a statement from the Secret Service. Anyway, that's all I know. I hope it helps."

"More than you realize," Ray said. "Any idea what the name of the agent in charge is?"

"Courtney Blaze," I said. "I don't know where she's staying, but she did say she'd be close by for the next few days." As I said that last bit, my timer went off. "Sorry, but we're out of time. Emma, are you ready to get back to work?"

"But I'm not finished yet," the newspaperman protested.

"Ray, there's honestly nothing else I can tell you." That wasn't true at all, but I was beginning to regret revealing the arrest, especially since I wasn't all that sure it had been a valid one to begin with.

"Fine," he said, slapping his notebook shut. "Thanks for your time." That last bit was said in a hard and robotic voice, and his level of sincerity was obviously pretty low.

"Dad," Emma said as she stood. "Thank her."

"I just did," Ray protested.

"Sure, but this time, try to sound as though you mean it," Emma insisted.

"You're right. I'm sorry." He turned back to me and added, "I really appreciate you taking the time to talk with me, Suzanne. I know how much your breaks with my daughter mean to the both of you."

"You're right there," I said with a smile. "Come on. Let's go," I said as I turned back to Emma.

"Right behind you, boss," Emma said. As she passed by her father, I saw her smile at him and reach out to touch his hand before she left him standing outside alone. I wouldn't have believed it, but she was actually managing to get her father to act a bit more civilized, though it was clear he still had a long way to go.

"Thanks for that," Emma said once we were back in the kitchen and she had added more hot water to the sink. "He means well. You know that, don't you?"

"Hey, he helped produce a daughter like you," I said with a slight grin. "In my book, that buys him quite a bit of goodwill."

"It's appreciated," she said. "Now let's make the rest of our donuts so our customers will be fat and happy by the end of the day."

"We're not responsible for *every* ounce of extra weight they put on," I told her.

"You know what I mean," she answered.

As we both got back to work, I found myself wondering just how long Agent Blaze would be in town and if she honestly believed she'd caught the real counterfeiter herself. I tried to imagine why she'd claim that if she didn't believe it, and then I realized that if she knew that she was dealing with someone crafty enough to spring her trap, they might be a little harder to catch than she first thought. If she arrested, or even held, Slick Willie for a while, maybe the counterfeiter would let his guard down and she could swoop in and catch the real crook.

At least that was what I hoped was happening.

Otherwise, I was afraid an innocent man was going to go to jail for a very long time for a crime he hadn't even committed.

It was six a.m., and we were ready to open the shop for the day. When I walked out front to turn the lights on and unlock the front door, I was surprised to see a familiar face standing there impatiently waiting for me to open.

At least she was familiar as of the day before.

"Did you change your mind about that free donut?" I asked Agent Blaze as she walked into Donut Hearts.

Emma had trailed behind me, but the moment she saw the agent's pained expression, my assistant ducked back into the kitchen before she had taken more than one step toward me.

"No donuts, no. I'm here on official business," she said curtly. "Did you or did you not tell one Ray Blake that we'd made an arrest in the counterfeiting case?"

"You told me that last night," I said in my own defense. "I just sort of assumed it was public knowledge."

"I told your husband in confidence, and I expected you to respect that," she said tersely.

"Then maybe you should have told me that as well," I said. "What's the harm? You got your man, right? Or did you?"

"What do you mean by that?" she asked me sharply.

"Just that if you're trying to lull the real culprit into dropping his guard, having it printed up in the newspaper might work in your favor, wouldn't it? Or am I completely wrong about you?"

Agent Blaze hesitated a bare second, and I knew that I never wanted to play poker with this woman. She was too good at hiding her true feelings. "I'm sure I don't know what you're talking about."

"That's too bad," I said.

"What is that supposed to mean?" she asked me sharply. "I've given you some leeway given your connections to Officer Bishop, but don't push it too far."

"It's just Jake these days, as you well know," I reminded her. "I never gave Ray a name. In fact, I told him to speak with you directly about the entire incident. I'm assuming he found you."

"I was having my breakfast at the Boxcar Grill, as a matter of fact," she said. "I didn't like being ambushed by a reporter like that."

"It's no fun, is it? I can't tell you the number of times he's done the same thing to me."

This woman clearly did not know how to take me. "I trust you'll be a little more discreet in the future?"

"We can always hope," I said without changing my expression.

Agent Blaze took that in for a moment, then she turned and walked out of my shop without saying another word. I briefly considered waving her down and shoving a bag of donuts and a cup of coffee into her hands, but in the end I decided that discretion was indeed the better part of valor.

It was a curious exchange, and I couldn't wait to talk to Jake about it, but there was no time to call him just yet.

Suddenly I had a crowd of people descending on my donut shop, and after all, that was why I was in business in the first place, to serve my customers and to take their money for the privilege.

Jake and I would talk later though, that much was certain.

I would probably get a lecture from him, too.

Some days it just didn't pay to try to do a good deed.

Chapter 7

"I CAN GUARANTEE YOU that particular twenty is good, Suzanne. It better be; I made it myself this morning," Harry Dale said as he handed me a twenty to pay for his morning treats and coffee. I did my best to offer a brief, if insincere smile, but it was the fourth time I'd heard it that morning, and it was already getting old. As I'd suspected, word had gotten out quickly about what we'd found at the flip house, and my customers weren't about to let it go without taking a shot or two at humor.

I pulled out my counterfeit testing pen and ran it across the bill, all the while smiling. "I must say, you do fine work."

Harry frowned for a moment. "I was just kidding, Suzanne. I'd never try to pass a counterfeit bill."

"I know that, Harry, but who knows where you got this one? With what's been going on around here, it just pays to be careful, don't you think?"

Harry pondered that as I gave him his change. After he took his change from me, he asked softly, "Where do you get one of those pens? Are they very expensive?"

"I bought mine at the hardware store," I told him. "It cost more than a regular pen, but then again, it only has to work once to more than pay for itself."

I had a hunch there was going to be a run on those pens in the next few days. We were all a little wary at the moment, even though it appeared that the counterfeiting was over. Who knew how many bills had already been spent, though? I planned on checking anything over a five for the next month, and I needed to remind Emma to do the same.

Grace came in as Harry left. It was good to see my best friend. "Coffee and a cruller?" It had become her usual order, at least for the moment.

"If you'll make it for the road," she said with a grimace. "I'm going out of town for a few days."

"Trouble?" I asked her. I knew her work was usually pretty undemanding, but there were times when she had to put in more hours than I did, if you counted her travel time, at any rate.

"No, we've got a conference on the Outer Banks." The OBX, as some folks called the chain of barrier islands off the coast of North Carolina, were beautiful, if becoming way overdeveloped. I remembered when I'd been a young girl and my folks had taken me there on vacation one summer. I'd been amazed by the miles and miles of open dunes along the coast, the sea grass waving in the constant breeze. The place had fascinated me. Jake and I had taken a brief vacation there a year ago, and I'd been stunned by the transformation. There may have still been stretches of pristine shorefront property in existence there, but if there were, we hadn't seen them. I didn't have any problem with progress per se, but I had missed the isolated beaches from my memory, replaced by house after house after house, all on stilts, all crammed in like sixteen donuts in a box meant to hold only twelve.

"You don't sound all that excited," I told her.

"I love the beach, but we're going to all be staying in some McMansion on the water with nine bedrooms. It's supposed to be a teambuilding exercise for the sales managers, but my best work-friend just left us for a competitor, and I don't really care for the rest of my coworkers."

"Why did she leave?"

"It wasn't just that the grass was greener on the other side. She's really good at what she does, and she's got ambition to burn. I wouldn't be surprised if she's running the place within a few years."

As I handed Grace her coffee and treat, she slid her money across the counter. I usually let her slide on paying me, but she always insisted, so lately I'd stopped fighting her. "Did you apply for the same position?"

"Me?" she asked with a hearty laugh. "Suzanne, I'm perfectly happy right where I am. I know what I'm doing, I'm good at it, and as long as my team keeps turning in good numbers, my bosses pretty much leave me alone. Why on earth would I want to advance up the corporate food chain? I've always believed that the higher you climb up the ladder, the more chance you have of people taking shots at you. Thank you very much, but I'm perfectly content right where I am."

"Well, I for one am happy you're hanging around," I said. "It's a long drive to the coast, isn't it?"

She groaned a little. "It's going to be even longer since I have to drive to Charlotte to pick my boss up at the airport. She's riding with me, so the seven-hour drive is going to feel like seven years. At least she's riding back with Mindi."

"I take it you're not a fan," I said.

"Of my boss, or of Mindi?" she asked. "Not so much, and the answer is the same on both counts. The things I do for a paycheck."

I thought about the endless hours I spent at Donut Hearts, the sleep I'd lost over the years since I'd bought the place, and the razor-thin margins I made from my labors. "Yeah, you've got it rough. I'd trade you dead even, but I'm not sure I could handle the strain of being you." I grinned at her as I said it, and she quickly returned it with a broad smile of her own.

"I know, it's definitely a first-world problem I've got." She shook the treat bag. "Thanks. I'll call you when I get back into town. We can have lunch at Napoli's."

"I'm holding you to that. I'll be here," I said. "Safe travels."

"Thanks," she said as she walked out.

"Where is Grace heading off to in such a hurry?" Mayor George Morris asked me as my best friend nearly ran him over.

"She's going to the Outer Banks," I said.

"For business or pleasure?" he asked me.

"Business, strictly business," I said. "What can I get you, Mr. Mayor?"

"I'll take a fritter and some coffee," George said. "Unlike your friend, I'm not in any hurry at all. The Council is breathing down my neck again about our budget, and I'm going to hide out here for a while, if it's all the same to you." He glanced at his watch as he added, "In about seven minutes, they're going to realize that I'm standing them up, and I want to sit here quietly, enjoy my goodies, and savor the experience."

I laughed as I filled his order. George sat at the counter by the register, and I was happy to catch up with my old friend. "You don't have to keep running for reelection if you're tired of being the mayor, you know. Let someone else take on your headaches."

He looked at me wistfully for a moment before he spoke. "I could just walk away from it all, couldn't I?"

"Just think, you could go fishing anytime you wanted and just laze around the rest of the time," I said, smiling.

"I've given it due consideration, trust me, but I'm worried retirement won't sit well with me. Remember, when I left the police force, I got so desperate for something to do that I even helped you investigate a murder or two."

"I thought you had fun, right up until the time you got hit by a suspect's car," I said. After all these years, it was finally something we'd both learned to joke about, though it had nearly cost him dearly at the time.

"Occupational hazard, it goes with the territory," he said with a shrug. "Do you need a full-time assistant these days?"

"Hey, that job's already been taken," Emma said from behind me. I hadn't even heard her come in from the kitchen, but she did that occasionally to collect the dirty dishes, cups, and glasses so we could serve the next group of customers that came into Donut Hearts.

"I don't want *your* job. Trust me," George told Emma.

She seemed mollified by his answer. "Good, because I'm not in any hurry to give it up."

"I was offering Suzanne my detecting skills," he explained.

"I thought that the counterfeiting case was already solved," Emma said, puzzled by his statement.

"I'm speaking in general terms," the mayor said, and as my assistant disappeared into the kitchen again, George asked, "Did they really already arrest the counterfeiter?"

"That's what they're claiming," I said guardedly.

"But you don't believe it," George pressed.

"Let's just say that I'm keeping an open mind," I answered.

He was about to follow up with another question when a well-dressed stranger approached the counter. "Excuse me. I'm looking for Suzanne Hart."

"Then this is your lucky day, because you just found her," I said, giving the man a smile. "What can I do for you?"

"It's what I can do for you, as a matter of fact. I'd like to buy your house."

Chapter 8

"PARDON ME?" I ASKED. "I'm not sure where you got your information, but my cottage is not for sale, not now, not ever."

He frowned as he idly played with a large round tarnished brass token in one hand. I noticed that it had the imprint of a lighthouse on one side, and I wondered what amusement park vending machine it had once belonged to. "Surely you can't be that attached to a place you bought only days ago," he said. "I'm sure we can work something out."

His true intent suddenly became clear. "Oh, you're talking about the flip. I don't own that. Well, at least not all of it. I have a fourth of it, to be exact." For some reason I felt the need to overexplain everything to this man. It wasn't just that he was handsome, though he was that, but he had a commanding presence that made me feel as though I couldn't bring myself to disappoint him for some odd reason.

"I understand that, but I went by the house early this morning, and no one was there. Then I tried to track the other owners of record down, but they were all nowhere to be found."

"Jake and Phillip were probably having breakfast or off buying supplies, and my mother is a hard woman to find on her best days," I explained. "The house we're all remodeling is not for sale, either, at least not yet."

"I assure you, I'll make certain you realize a healthy profit from the transaction. I can make it quick and fruitful for you all."

"I'm curious about something. If you want the place so badly, why didn't you just offer more for it than we paid? We just bought it a few days ago."

His expression clouded over. "Unfortunately, I was called away out of town unexpectedly. I had been under the impression that I had a deal with the owner when I left, so imagine my chagrin when I came back and found that the title had already been transferred to someone else."

"Or in our case, someones else." I knew it wasn't proper grammar, but it made me smile, so I said it anyway. There were more important things in life than following the stylebooks of proper English syntax. "I'm sorry you feel as though you were treated badly in the deal, but we bought it fair and square. We're taking it down to the studs and remodeling it from top to bottom before we put it back on the market, so if you can just be a little patient, it will be on the market again if you're still interested later."

"That's not going to be good enough," he said as he pulled out a checkbook. "I'm afraid I must insist. I'll pay you more than you'll make from flipping it, but it has to be right now. Call your partners and get them over here. I want this over and done by lunchtime today."

I grinned at him. "You know, there may be some people that quiver and faint at the sight of your stern expression, but none of us are in that group. We don't take kindly to bullying, no matter what form it might take."

"I'm not bullying you," he said, the frustration clear in both his voice and his expression. "You're not acting rationally. Call them and at least give me the opportunity to talk sense to the rest of the people in your party."

George spoke up at that point. Evidently he'd had enough. "You heard the lady. The place is not for sale."

The stranger turned to look at my friend harshly. "And who exactly are you, and what business is any of this of yours?"

George stood and got within six inches of the man's face. I saw him blanch a bit, but to his credit, he held his ground.

"I'm the mayor, and she's my friend. Now don't make me say it again. It's time you took off."

The stranger shook his head, and then I saw the most remarkable transition in expressions blossom on his face. Going from perturbed to pleasant in an instant, he instead offered his hand to George with a bright smile. "I'm afraid we've gotten off on the wrong foot. Please allow me to introduce myself. I'm Lionel Henderson III."

"George Morris," the mayor said as he took the man's hand warily. "Like she said, though, the place is not for sale."

"Of course. I understand. This isn't the time or the place to discuss my proposition. Sorry to bother you, Ms. Hart," he told me before leaving.

"That was a bit harsh, even for you," I told George after Henderson was gone.

"The man was too pushy, and way too slick for my tastes," the mayor said. "I don't trust him."

"Wow, that was a bad first impression he made on you, wasn't it? I admit that I didn't care for his demeanor either, but I didn't want to throw him out into the street the moment he walked in."

"I was just looking out for you," George said softly.

I walked over to him and put my hands on his shoulders, then I looked him squarely in the eye. "George, you are one of my dearest friends in the world, but you of all people should know that I can take care of myself. Now, don't you have a meeting with the council that you need to get to?"

He grumbled a little until I kissed his cheek gently. That made him blush, which was my intention in the first place. "I just didn't want to see you get steamrolled," the mayor said. It was the best apology I could have expected.

"Did you honestly think that was ever going to happen?" I asked him.

He laughed at that, and all was well between us again. "Not likely."

"You bet it won't."

George nodded. "I guess I can't put it off anymore. If I don't at least go make an appearance, I'll never hear the end of it. If you need me, I'll be in my office."

"Keeping April Springs safe and prosperous, I trust," I told him.

"Sure, why not? If thinking that helps you sleep at night, then more power to you."

After George was gone, I thought about Henderson's offer. I had to agree with the mayor. There was something not quite right about it, and I couldn't wait to discuss it with my other partners in our house-flipping venture.

It would have to wait, though.

For now I had donuts to sell and coffee to pour.

My customers needed me, and I was going to do everything in my power to make their visit to Donut Hearts a good one.

To my surprise, Jake walked in an hour later. He looked grim, and I had to wonder what had happened to change his early buoyant mood. "Suzanne, you need to come to the house with me right now."

"Why? What happened?"

"I'll tell you along the way. Can Emma cover for you?"

"Of course, but Jake, I need to know what's going on."

"We had a break-in," he said.

After I got Emma set up, I followed Jake out to his truck. "Should I follow you there?"

"No, I'll bring you right back, but I wanted you to see this before I called Chief Grant."

I was really getting worried now, but I didn't quite understand. "Jake, there wasn't anything to steal, was there? You took your tools with you yesterday, and the appliances were already in the dumpster. They didn't take the wiring, did they?"

"No, but then again, it's not copper; it's aluminum. That's why we're going to rewire it."

I knew that there had been a rash of thefts from new homes where thieves would move into a house under construction and steal the wiring just to take it to a salvage yard.

"What exactly of value was there for them to take?" I asked.

"It's not what they took," he explained. "It's what they left."

"Okay, I'm really not following you now. Are you saying that some-one broke into the house we're flipping and *left* something? It doesn't make any sense."

"It was blood, Suzanne. Evidently whoever broke in got injured be-fore they managed to get back out."

"I don't understand," I said, more confused than ever.

"Neither do we, but Phillip and I agreed that you and Dot had a right to see the scene before we called the police. It's not like getting Chief Grant there any sooner is going to change anything. Whatever happened is long over," he said.

I kept peppering him with questions for the rest of the short drive, but he had no more answers for me, so I finally decided to just wait and see it for myself. As we drove up to the house, I saw the curtains of Cur-tis's house suddenly close. Evidently he was keeping tabs on the comings and goings of our house-remodeling project, but we didn't have time to deal with him at the moment.

When I walked to the front door, Jake put a restraining hand on my shoulder. "I don't want to contaminate what very well could be an ac-tive crime scene," he explained. "I've been through the house, so I know that there are no bodies here. I suppose that's something, anyway. If you don't mind, stay right where you are."

I did as he asked and looked inside from my vantage point near the door. I was surprised not only by the obvious blood present near a neat stack of two-by-fours but also by how clean the place was otherwise. The dumpster outside was gone, and I had to wonder if Agent Blaze had confiscated it, along with everything else in the house that hadn't been nailed down. It looked as though they'd even vacuumed the floor in their search for clues. It was all in stark contrast with the bloody drops leading out the back door.

Clearly something had happened here.

"Did whoever break in cut themselves on some glass?" I asked as I looked around for a point of entry.

"No. The back door was kicked in, but there was never any glass in it to begin with. In fact, everything is intact as far as that goes. None of the windows were even cracked."

"Then what happened?" I asked him.

"If you look closely, you can spot an occasional spattering of blood besides what's on the wall over there, so whoever was injured managed to get out under their own power."

"Or they were dragged out," I said with a shudder.

"I don't think so. If they'd been dragged, there would be a completely different set of bloodstains we'd be dealing with right now," he said matter-of-factly. It was clear that my husband had seen that before in his previous incarnation as a state police investigator.

Phillip showed up just then with Momma in tow. She took one glance inside and then stepped away without prodding. "This house is turning out to be cursed, isn't it?" she asked in a throaty whisper.

"Dot, you can't blame the house," Phillip said, and then he turned to me. "What do you think about this, Suzanne?"

"I'm still taking it in, but I agree with you. I don't think it's cursed. This has to be related to the counterfeiting somehow."

Jake frowned. "Why do you say that?"

"I doubt this was random," I told him. "My guess is that two partners had a falling out when they discovered that the money was gone, and one thing led to another."

"I suppose that it's possible," Jake answered.

"It's also feasible that this was just a pair of hobos looking for a place to stay when they got into a fight," my stepfather said.

"You don't actually believe that, do you?" I asked him.

"The truth is that we just don't know," Phillip replied.

"Well, regardless of what really happened, we need to call Chief Grant," I said as I reached for my cell phone. "Unless any of you have any objections to that."

"As a matter of fact, I do," Agent Blaze said as she stepped out into the light.

## Chapter 9

"HOW LONG HAVE YOU BEEN standing there?" I asked her.

"Long enough," she said. "We had this place under surveillance all night, but there was no sign of anyone. I left one of my agents around the corner to keep an eye on things, but he fell asleep while whatever happened here occurred."

I looked around and saw that there was only one agent standing behind her now, and I didn't have to guess the fate of the one who'd literally fallen asleep on the job. No doubt he was heading back to the home office to clean out his desk and start polishing up his resumé for his next position as a dog walker.

"So, you knew about this how long, exactly?" Jake asked.

"We found it just before you and Phillip arrived the first time," she said.

"Why didn't you tell us about it then?"

"Frankly, I wanted to see if whoever did this would come back. I was about to come forward when you two left again, so I decided to bide my time in case the suspects came back."

Something clicked in my mind just then. "So, you suspect there's more than meets the eye here too, don't you? I was right after all."

Blaze shrugged me off. "I'm not at liberty to comment on an active investigation."

"Ah ha!" I said with a gleam in my eye.

"Ah ha what?" Momma asked me.

"It's still an active investigation, which means Agent Blaze here doesn't believe that Slick Willie is behind this any more than I am," I said, trying to at least tone down my triumphant response.

"Let's just say that it all seemed a little too pat to us," the Secret Service agent admitted. "I decided that it might be prudent to appear to buy the setup and see what happened."

It must have been hard for her to admit, so I decided to quit while I was ahead. "What happens now?"

"We step back in," she said. "I'm afraid this will delay your work again. Whatever they were here looking for was evidently important enough to commit an assault, if not a murder." It was a chilling thought, but I didn't have any time to comment as she added, "We need more time to do a more thorough examination of the property this time around."

"You haven't checked the kitchen area out thoroughly, have you?" Jake asked her solemnly.

"Jackson checked it," she said as she pointed to her remaining agent. "Why?"

"I didn't see anything amiss," the other agent said immediately.

"You wouldn't, unless you'd been working here earlier. There's an oversized vent cover that's not where it was before," Jake answered.

"Show me," she said.

The two of them started to walk in, and I tried to follow, only to be shut down. "I want to see, too," I protested. "If *you're* going to contaminate the crime scene, I don't see why I shouldn't be able to as well."

"We've already photographed the house, but Jake knows where and where not to step," she explained.

"Fine. The rest of us will wait right here." I said it as though I had a vote in the matter, even though it was clear that I didn't.

That didn't mean that I couldn't watch, though. I left the front door and walked around to the kitchen window. Once I was stationed there, I peered inside through the muck and the dust. Those windows were in need of a major cleaning, but that wasn't exactly my priority at the moment. I felt someone breathing on my neck and turned to see that Momma and Phillip had joined me for a better view of the action, though Agent Jackson must have remained at his post up front.

Jake walked directly to one wall and knelt down as he pulled a pair of latex gloves from his back pocket. Clearly Agent Blaze wasn't even surprised by the move, since she was doing the same thing herself. He pointed, she took some photos, and then after she nodded her permission, Jake carefully pulled the loose cover from the wall. The opening was the size of a briefcase, and I wondered if it might not be the return air duct for the furnace.

Inside a space that appeared to lead to nowhere, I could see that the area between the stud walls had been recently converted into a hiding place. I couldn't hear what they were saying, but one look at the expression on Agent Blaze's face told me that she was angry with herself and the agents under her that they'd missed it on their earlier search. Jake tried to console her, but she wouldn't have it, and soon enough he was leaving the house by the front door. We all raced around to speak with him, but once he was back outside, he just shook his head and motioned for us to step away from Agent Jackson so we could talk.

"Did you know that hiding space was there all along?" I asked him in a whisper the second we were far enough away to have a quiet conversation without being overheard.

"I didn't have a clue, but we would have found it very soon. That's clearly why it was a priority to break back into the house and take whatever they'd been hiding there."

"So, you believe it was the counterfeiters, too?" I asked him.

Instead of answering me directly, he turned to Phillip. "I do. There's just too much evidence to make me think otherwise."

"I agree. Based on what we know now, I believe that Suzanne is right."

I normally couldn't hear that enough in the course of a day, but it was no time to dwell on my small victory. "What could it have been that they were after?"

"Who knows? More counterfeit money? If this was twenty years ago, I'd think it might have held printing press plates, but with the sophistication of laser printers these days, those aren't necessary. You can get a pretty amazing copy with a little practice."

"That may be true, but passable paper is still a necessary part of the operation," I said. "How do you fake those holograms and metallic strips?"

"I don't think you do," Jake said, "but what do I know? That was never my area of expertise. I'm guessing that whoever was making these didn't count on anyone doing even the simplest checks." Jake hit his head with his hand. "I can't believe it. I'm an idiot."

"Don't talk about my husband that way," I protested. "He's the smartest man I know."

"The discarded bills we found were all of the new design that normally have the precautions built into them," Jake said.

"So?" Momma asked.

"They were the discards. I'm sure of it. My guess is that whoever made them realized they couldn't pass the simplest test, so they started making the only bills worth trying to replicate these days, the old-style ones. I'm guessing *that's* going to be the real flood of counterfeit bills."

"It's all just theory though, isn't it? Aren't you giving whoever did this too much credit?"

"No, I'm beginning to think this was their plan all along," Jake said as he frowned.

"Why go to the trouble of arousing anyone's suspicion with the new bills if they were planning on making the old ones all along?"

"Think about it. Everyone is going to be looking for phony new bills while the counterfeiter is quietly making stacks of the old design. Plus, what if they'd planned to get rid of any partners they had from the very start? Having those new fakes on hand would be a perfect way to plant them on their co-conspirators without raising too much alarm about what they were really up to. In fact, I'm willing to guess that they are making hundreds in the old design, not twenties. That would further distance what they were really doing from everyone, including the people they were working with."

"If that's the case," Phillip said, "why send Slick Willie in? Surely you don't suspect him of being part of this ring."

"No, but what if whoever our master counterfeiter tried to set up wouldn't take the bait? They still needed the trap sprung, so they went to Plan B."

"I don't know," Momma said. "Jake, forgive me for saying so, but it all seems a bit too farfetched to me."

"I know," Jake said as he shook his head. "What's more, it's going to be extremely hard to prove."

"I wouldn't even know how to go about it," I said. "Do you?"

"We can ask around for someone who's missing, or maybe just injured, and see if we can trace it back that way," he admitted, "but I'm sure Agent Blaze is going to cover that base, especially after missing whatever was stashed in that hideaway yesterday."

"Do you honestly think that was her fault?" Momma asked him. I'd wondered the same thing myself. She couldn't be expected to cover every detail, could she?

"Without a doubt. I'm sure she turned the place back over to us prematurely because of our past re...acquaintance." He'd clearly been about to say relationship, but I had to give him points for at least trying to backtrack.

"So what do we do now?" Phillip asked my husband.

"I'm not at all certain that there's anything we can do," Jake said. "It's out of our hands."

"Then we go back to what we were planning to do before," I told them. "Jake, you and Phillip continue your planning until she releases the house again, while Momma and I both go back to work until this all gets sorted out."

Jake looked at me incredulously. "Do you honestly think you can do that, just walk away and let someone else handle the investigation?"

"Of course not," I said as I shook my head. "I'm far too curious a creature to just leave it to the feds. We need to dig into this, but around the edges, not at the heart of the matter."

"How do you propose we do that? I'm not disagreeing, I'm just curious."

"When I figure that out, I'll let you know, but there's one place we can start," I said.

"Where's that?" Momma asked me curiously.

"There's a man named Lionel Henderson III who offered to buy this place this morning for far more than it's worth. I believe we should go see him and find out why."

"I know him," Momma said guardedly. "If you're trying to catch him off guard, I'd better not go with you, at least not at first. Besides, the four of us would overwhelm him if we descended on him all at once."

Phillip said, "You and Jake should handle it, Suzanne. I need to get Dot back to April Springs."

"Thanks," Jake said, not hiding his gratitude for the offer.

"That's not really fair though, is it? Why should Phillip be left out?" Momma asked. She looked at me before adding, "No offense, Suzanne, but my husband is also a trained law enforcement officer."

I could appreciate the fact that Momma was standing up for her husband, but I wasn't entirely sure how to answer it when once again Phillip stepped up. "Dot, it just makes sense. He approached Suzanne at the donut shop. It's only natural she'd bring her husband along to pursue the conversation."

My mother studied him for a moment and then must have finally decided that it made sense enough given the context, and I mouthed a silent "thank you" to my stepfather. He merely grinned in return, something that Momma caught. "What are you two carrying on about?"

"Us?" I asked her as innocently as I could muster. "Nothing, nothing at all. Why do you ask?"

Clearly unsatisfied with my answer, she turned to her husband. "Phillip?"

Instead of replying, he simply took his wife's arm. "Let's get you home, shall we? We can discuss it on the way."

"Very well," Momma said, "but you had better believe that discuss it we shall." There was no playfulness in her voice as she said it, and Phillip clearly heard it.

After they left us, I asked, "Are you okay with it being just the two of us?"

"Are you kidding? That's my favorite combination. Any chance you know how to find this man Henderson?"

"No, but I have a hunch I know someone who will." I suddenly remembered that I was nearly out of gas in the Jeep. "How's your gas?"

"I just topped it off yesterday. Why do you ask?"

"You should probably drive, then. What do you think about going to Napoli's?"

"I wasn't planning to stop for lunch first, but I'm game if you are. Are they even open yet?"

"Is that all you can think about, your stomach?" I asked him with a smile. "They aren't officially open to the public, but I have a hunch Angelica will open the kitchen door in back if she knows it's us."

"You, you mean," Jake replied.

"Us," I insisted.

"So, let me get this straight. We're going to what might possibly be the best Italian restaurant in the entire South just to ask questions about a case we're digging into?" His disappointment was palpable.

"That's the main reason, but if she offers to feed us, don't say no."

He looked at me in shock. "Is that even a possibility in your mind?"

"No," I said with a hint of laughter. "It's not. Just remember that eating is not the main reason we're going to Napoli's."

"Hey, as long as it's any part of the motivation, I'm on board. Do you really think Angelica will know where we can find Lionel Henderson?"

"If she doesn't, I'm willing to bet that she'll know someone who does," I said confidently. "Between her and her daughters, they're like a secret spy network."

"A secret spy network that feeds you," Jake corrected me.

"That, too," I said as we got into his truck and started toward Union Square.

It was time to call in reinforcements, and I had a feeling we were going to exactly the right people who might be able to help us out.

# Chapter 10

"YOU'RE LATE," ANGELICA DeAngelis said as she opened the door before she even saw that it was us.

"That's funny, I didn't even realize that you were expecting us," I said with a smile.

"Suzanne! Jake! What a pleasant surprise. My supplier, on the other hand, is going to get heartily scolded, that is if he ever decides to show up. Come in."

"Thanks. Sorry we're here before you open," I said as Jake and I stepped inside the kitchen area. The restaurant itself might not be open yet, but the aromas coming from the back were amazing. The youngest daughter, Sophia, nodded in our direction, but she was hunched over a pot of what looked to be marinara sauce, and I was pretty sure she was watching to make sure that it didn't burn. Sophia might have been the youngest of Angelica's daughters, but she'd become nearly as good as her mother in the kitchen, which was really saying something. The other girls helped out occasionally, but mostly they ran the front and let their mother and youngest sibling deal with the majority of the work in the kitchen.

"You two are always welcome here. You know that," Angelica said with a grin. "Sophia, aren't you even going to look up long enough to say hello to our friends?"

Sophia looked up and grinned at us. "Hello," she said before going back to her pot.

Angelica smiled softly. "That one is worse than me sometimes."

"Hey, I heard that," Sophia said.

"Good, I meant you to," she said. "Are you hungry?" she asked as she turned back to us. "I might be able to whip something together for you."

Jake was about to agree when I stopped him. We were there for a reason, and it wasn't to eat. Well, not *just* to eat, anyway. "Angelica, do you know a man named Lionel Henderson?"

Her face clouded immediately. "Yes, I know Number Three."

"Is that what you call him?" I asked.

"Just behind his back," she assured me. "One and Two come in as well, but Three is a fixture around here. No matter how bad the service we give him is, no matter how close we seat him to the restroom, he continues to insist on dining with us."

"Why the icy treatment?" I asked.

Angelica looked a little pained. "I know, it's not like me, but there's something about that entire family that leaves me cold."

"I don't know the father or grandfather," I said sympathetically, "but if they're anything like the son, they probably feel entitled to get whatever it is they want, and when you refuse them, they act like petulant children."

"That's it exactly," Angelica said as she laughed and clapped her hands together. She turned to Jake. "You, sir, married very well."

"You don't have to tell me that," Jake said with a grin.

"So, where might we find him?" I asked her.

"He's bound to be in his office, though what exactly he does I do not know. The door says Speculation and Development, but I'm sure it's just a front for something shady."

"Why do you say that?" Jake asked her. He was, if nothing else, a student of human nature, and the workings of the mind never ceased to fascinate him.

"He's always looking to profit from his actions at someone else's expense," she said. "I could tell you stories about him if you need proof, but trust me; you can take my word for it."

"We have absolute faith in you, Angelica," I told her. "Where exactly might his office be?"

"Do you *really* have to go see him?" she asked us, a worried expression crossing her face.

"It's important. At least it could be," I said, hedging my bets a little. After all, we didn't know for sure that he'd had anything to do with what had happened at our flip house earlier. Then again, he was just about the only viable suspect we had at the moment, so we honestly had no choice but to brace him in his den, no matter how unpleasant that might turn out to be.

"Would you at least like a bite to fortify you first?" she asked.

I was tempted, especially with the aromas that were enveloping us, but the puritan work ethic was too strong in me. "Would you mind if we came back by *after* we talked to him?" I asked her.

"Suzanne, what would it hurt to grab a bite first?" Jake asked as he looked around the kitchen like a kid in a candy store.

I couldn't bring myself to refuse him. "Angelica, are you *sure* we won't be in the way?"

"Nonsense. You are family. You *can't* be in the way."

Antonia had walked into the kitchen and had listened to the last part of our conversation. "That's not what you told me last night, Mom."

Angelica turned to her daughter. "That's because you were in the bathroom much longer than you needed to be."

"There are other bathrooms in our house," Antonia protested.

"But mine has the best bathtub," her mother countered.

"Why do you think she used it?" Sophia chimed in, grinning as she spoke.

"Don't you have some sauce to watch?" Angelica asked her pointedly.

"I can do both," Sophia said. "Besides, Antonia had a date. She needed a good place to get ready."

"Not that I approve of the young man she went out with," Angelica said.

"Mom, is there *any* man good enough for one of your daughters?" Antonia asked as she kissed her mother's cheek.

"Now that you mention it, no." She paused a moment and then looked squarely at Jake. "Why can't you girls find someone like Jake?"

"Sorry, but he's spoken for," I said as I put my arm around my husband's shoulders.

"Why do I suddenly feel like a piece of meat?" Jake asked, clearly bemused by the situation.

"Stop protesting. You love it and you know it," I told him.

"I never denied it," Jake replied with a grin.

"Jacob, don't you have any friends for my daughters?" Angelica asked him.

"None that are good enough for them," my husband answered honestly.

That got a reaction he hadn't expected when Sophia put down her wooden spoon and she and her sister approached Jake from either side and kissed his cheeks. I laughed when I saw him blush slightly.

"You two are making the poor man uncomfortable," Angelica told her daughters.

"I don't mind," Jake said.

I had to laugh again. "I don't either, but let's not make a habit of it. I'd hate for him to get used to the kind of attention only you two can give him."

Antonia smiled. "You have nothing to worry about with us. The man never takes his eyes off of you. You are lucky to have him."

"I feel lucky," I said.

"Besides, I've given up men," Sophia said with a shrug. "I'm going to focus on my cooking instead."

Angelica approached her youngest and put her arm around her. "You'll find love again."

"What happened?" I asked.

"A young man in town decided of his own accord not to see my darling little girl anymore. Can you imagine it?"

"What an idiot," Jake blurted out without thinking.

Sophia grinned at him. "Jake, are you trying to get another kiss from me?"

"No, no thanks, not that it wouldn't be appreciated. No. No. No thanks," he stammered.

"Suzanne, he's absolutely adorable, isn't he?" Sophia asked me with a conspiratorial grin.

"There's no doubt about it in my mind," I replied.

"Enough teasing Jake, ladies. Let me get you two plates." Angelica took two dinner plates and started to heap them up with food. I felt my mouth watering at the very sight of mine as she placed it in front of me, and I realized that Jake had been right. *Nothing* was worth delaying an experience like this for.

"This is amazing," Jake said after swallowing another bite of his sampler platter. "I can't imagine anything ever being any better."

"Suzanne's donuts are pretty magical, too," Sophia said. "You don't happen to have any with you, do you?"

I shook my head. "Sorry. I left the shop early, and chances are good that Emma took whatever was left for her class at college."

"How's she doing?" Sophia asked.

"Very nicely. She somehow manages to work with me, go to college, *and* date Barton, all at the same time," I reported between bites.

"That makes me exhausted just thinking about it," Angelica said with a sigh.

"You're no slouch yourself," I said. "You and your girls run this place brilliantly."

"Honestly, it's become second nature for us," she said.

"How's *your* love life?" I asked her. "Have you had any big dates lately?"

"Mom? You're kidding, right? She's married to this place these days," Sophia said with a grin.

"As are you," Angelica reminded her youngest daughter. "For now, it's enough."

"But not forever, right, Mom?" Maria asked. I'd been so focused on my meal that I hadn't even seen her come in. The lasagna was the best it had ever been, but I was afraid to ask which DeAngelis had made it. I didn't want Sophia to get cocky about it, or to feel bad if it had come from her mother's hands. Either way, I could live off the stuff, breakfast, lunch, and dinner.

"Not forever," Angelica said before brushing off any further comments or questions about her love life. "How is your meal?"

"These are without a doubt the best things I've ever eaten in my life," Jake said. "Sorry," he added as he turned to me.

"If you had said anything different, I would have thought you were either lying or completely crazy," I answered with a smile. "I'm not sure I'm going to be able to do anything after this but take a nap."

"I'm afraid that's not in the cards today," Jake said as he reluctantly pushed his empty plate away.

I knew in my heart that it was time to go, so I did the same thing myself. We couldn't put it off any longer. It was time to leave the warm, familiar embrace of Napoli's and go back out into the real world. At least we were doing it with high spirits, not to mention happy bellies. Angelica had refused payment for the meal, which I'd expected, and I was proud when Jake accepted her offer gracefully.

We got back into the truck and headed off on our quest to find the man who had shown so much interest in the flip property, and I found myself hoping that *this* case would be simple to solve, unlike the others I'd tackled in the past.

I had a feeling I was being more than a tad too optimistic, but there was only one way to find out, and that was to jump right in with both feet.

After riding in Jake's truck for a few minutes to the location in town Angelica had given us, we found a luxury sedan parked in front of the office. The license plate on it read LIH III, so I had a hunch Lionel Henderson III was inside. Jake glanced into the front and back seats as we passed by the car.

"Are you looking for something in particular?" I asked him.

"Just checking things out," Jake said. "It's more force of habit than anything."

"Are you armed, by any chance?" I asked him, though I hadn't seen any sign of a weapon on him. My husband had made more than his share of enemies in his past career, and I knew that he often left the house with a weapon, just in case. It was a constant reminder of the life he'd led before he'd left the force and joined me in April Springs.

"I am," he said as he gestured to his shoulder. "I hope you don't mind."

"Of course I don't," I answered. I had suspected as much, since Jake was wearing a light windbreaker even when he didn't need one. After all, there was no need for him to advertise the fact that he was going around armed.

"Why do you ask?"

"I was just checking," I said. The truth was that I had a feeling in my gut that things could go very wrong with this case very quickly, and it reassured me knowing that we weren't completely defenseless.

Lionel Henderson looked surprised when he answered his door, and more than a bit unhappy to find me standing on his office's doorstep with my husband.

## Chapter 11

"WHAT ARE YOU DOING here? How did you even find me?" he asked as he reluctantly stepped aside and let us into his small office. I noticed that the ever-present token was still in his hand, though he'd stopped playing with it the moment he saw us.

"Union Square isn't that large a town. You weren't very hard to track down," I said. "This is my husband, Jake Bishop, and one of my other partners."

Jake offered his hand, and Henderson reluctantly took it, albeit briefly. "Ms. Hart, I'm afraid you've wasted a trip."

"We ate at Napoli's, so there's no way this trip could ever be considered wasted," I said. "Why do I get the sudden feeling that you are no longer interested in buying our flip house?"

"You're more perceptive than I gave you credit for," he said. "I'm afraid the deal is off."

"Wow, that was fast. May I ask why you changed your mind so suddenly?"

"My backer decided to go with another property when I couldn't reach an agreement with your group this morning," he said. "I'm afraid in this game, sometimes timing is everything."

"It wouldn't have anything to do with the fact that someone broke into the house not long after you left the donut shop, would it?" Jake asked him pointedly.

Both Henderson and I were shocked by the abruptness of his question, for two very different reasons. The businessman looked surprised as to what Jake was implying, while I was trying to wrap my head around his sudden, and very direct, approach. That was more like Grace, which may have been a good thing. Sometimes I took my own sweet time getting to the heart of the matter, dipping a toe in around the edges, whereas they favored leaping in with both feet. Both approaches could be valid, so it was good that we complemented each other, in more ways than one.

"What are you talking about?" Henderson asked a half beat too late to sound convincing, at least to me. "Someone broke into your house?"

"And took something they must have treasured very much to risk being caught taking it," I said. Since Jake had already broken the ice, I decided that I wanted to get in on the fun as well. There was something exhilarating about throwing caution to the wind like that.

"I can't imagine anything in that house being of value to anyone," he said brusquely.

"Can't you? Did you know about the counterfeiting ring that was going on there?" Jake asked him.

Wow, he was spilling things left and right! I wasn't sure I would have risked Agent Blaze's ire, but then again, Jake knew her much better than I did.

"Now you're just talking nonsense," Henderson said after a brief pause. Was he hiding his real reaction again, or was this just his habit of speaking? I didn't know him well enough to say, even though this was the second conversation I'd had with the man since meeting him earlier that morning.

"It's true enough," I said. "Who exactly is this mystery backer you referred to earlier?"

That didn't take a moment of thinking for him to answer. "I'm not at liberty to disclose that. Our business relationship is of a confidential nature. I'm sure you understand." Jake was about to ask him a follow-up question when he glanced at the clock on the wall behind him. "I'm afraid I'm going to have to cut this short. I have an important meeting I must attend to."

"Really? Where are you going? Maybe we can tag along," I suggested with my brightest fake smile.

"Thank you for the offer, but no, that wouldn't be at all appropriate. Now, if you'll excuse me," he said as he walked us to his door and opened it.

There wasn't much opportunity to stay after he basically threw the two of us out. Oh, well. That was one of the hazards of investigating anything, I'd found. If you couldn't take a few slammed doors in your face or heavily veiled threats, you shouldn't start digging into other people's lives.

Before we could leave though, he said, "Now that you mention it, I did see someone skulking around the building this morning when I came there looking for you."

"Really? Was it someone you recognized?" Jake asked him, poised to leap on another possible angle for us to investigate.

"Yes, I knew exactly who it was. It was Maxine Halliday. Do you know her?"

"Not personally, but I know of her," I admitted. "She runs her own realty company in town, right?"

"Yes, it's called Ultra Elite Prime Properties Real Estate," he said. "I thought it odd, and I called out to her, but instead of acknowledging me, she ducked behind the house and vanished into the woods. It was strange behavior, even for her."

"Thanks, we'll talk to her," I said. "Did you happen to see anyone else?"

"No, she was the only one," he said.

Feeling a strike of sudden inspiration, I asked him, "Do you happen to know a man named William Joseph Branch?"

"No, the name doesn't sound familiar," he answered promptly enough.

"They call him Slick Willie around town," I added.

That was a direct hit. Henderson took more than a second before he answered. "I've heard the name, but we've never met. Now I really must insist that you go. I can't afford to miss this meeting. Good day. Sorry we couldn't do business."

"I am, too," Jake said. "If you change your mind, you know where to find us."

After we backed out in the parking lot, I asked my husband, "Would you really sell the place right after buying it? You're not losing your nerve, are you? If you are, I won't judge you for it, I promise."

"Of course not. It's been too much fun so far," Jake said with a smile. "I just wanted to keep an avenue of communication open with him. He's lying to us about something," my husband added as he looked back at the office.

"Do you have any idea what exactly that might be?" I asked, honestly curious if my husband's reaction to Lionel Henderson was the same as mine had been.

"That's the question, isn't it? Suzanne, would you do me a favor?"

"You know that I'd do anything for you," I said.

"Are you sure you don't want to qualify that?" he asked me with a short grin.

"Positive. I would do anything and everything you asked of me, including helping you bury a body, if it came to that."

"Did you have any body in particular in mind?" he asked.

"I don't know, nor do I need to. Just tell me where to dig, hand me a shovel, and get out of my way."

Jake took a moment to look at me deeply. "I'm not sure whether I should be worried or honored."

"Can't it be a little bit of both? What can I do?"

"Stand by that door and don't let him out," Jake said as he hurried toward his truck.

"Ever?" I asked.

"No, just until I check something," Jake said.

"You've got it," I answered and took up a position by the door, ready to stop Lionel Henderson with whatever means I had at my disposal.

If he came out of his office, I was going to be ready for him.

When Jake came back from the truck, he had a high-powered flashlight in one hand and a large black canvas bag in the other. I'd seen him check it occasionally, so I knew that it contained spray bottles full of strange concoctions, long swabs, evidence bags, and a host of other things that served as his portable crime lab. It didn't surprise me at all that he was prepared to investigate just about anything, given his background. This may have been the first time he was going to be able to use it in one of our investigations, and I could swear that I caught him smiling as he pulled on a pair of latex gloves and squatted down by the door handle.

The smile turned abruptly to a frown, though. "I don't believe this."

"What's going on?" I asked him. "Should I come over there and join you?"

"You might as well," he said with disgust as he dabbed at a wet patch under the car door. "Smell this."

"It's bleach," I said as I recoiled. "You could have warned me." The strong acrid smell was unmistakable. I didn't normally use it at the donut shop or at home if I could help it. It was just too powerful for my taste.

"Sorry." Jake took off his glove and touched the surface of the car under the handle. "It's here, too."

"Why would he use *bleach* on his car? Especially one as nice as this?"

"Bleach is commonly used to destroy blood evidence, or at least make it tougher to work with. If he'd used oxidizing bleach, he wouldn't have risked damaging his paint job, but I'm guessing that he didn't know about that, so he used what he could find at the grocery store."

"Do you think that was *his* blood at the house?" I asked him. I hadn't seen a mark on him, but that didn't mean he couldn't have disguised a wound somehow.

"I don't know, but I'm about to ask him," Jake said.

Jake carried his bag and flashlight to the door, and then he used the butt of the light to knock heavily on it.

There was no response, so he knocked even harder, but Lionel Henderson III was clearly not in the mood to talk to us anymore.

"What about the important meeting he threw us out for so he could attend?" I asked Jake as we walked back to his truck.

"I'm guessing there never was a meeting in the first place," he said with disgust.

After we both got back into the truck, I asked my husband, "What are we going to do, wait around here all afternoon for him to come out?"

"No, not when we've got another lead. Let's assume for the moment that there's an innocent explanation for everything we've seen and heard here. Where does that leave us? Maxine Halliday. Do you feel like tackling her?"

"Why not? Do you think we'll have any more luck with her than we did with good old Lionel?"

"I hope so, but at least she'll have some motivation to speak with us," Jake said.

"Why is that?"

"Haven't you heard? We might be interested in selling the flip house," Jake said with a grin. "At least that's what we're going to tell her."

"Are you comfortable lying to her?" I asked my husband. I would have had little trouble doing it on my own, and I knew that Grace normally welcomed every opportunity to spin her own yarn, but my husband had an irritatingly strong sense of integrity that sometimes got in the way of uncovering the truth.

"I won't be lying," he said easily as he started the truck and started driving. "After all, we *will* be selling the place. It's just a matter of the timing that I'm going to hedge."

"And you can live with that?"

"If it helps us move our investigation forward, I can," he said.

"Well, all right then. Let's go see if Maxine is in her office."

Chapter 12

THE DOOR TO THE REAL estate office was unlocked, so evidently we were in luck. A smart-looking woman in her midfifties was sitting behind a massive desk with the nameplate MAXINE HALLIDAY sitting front and center. The most noticeable thing about her was the large floppy hat she wore, pulled down on one side enough to nearly cover one eye. I wouldn't have worn that hat under gunpoint, but she seemed comfortable enough with it, even if it did nearly obscure her vision out of one eye. Maxine was reading something fascinating on her laptop computer. Whether it was business or personal I couldn't say, since the screen was turned away from us. As Jake and I walked in, she immediately shut her laptop with a slam, making me wonder what exactly she'd been reading about.

"Hello. Welcome to Ultra Elite Prime Properties Real Estate," she said, offering Jake her hand. She shook mine as well, though not nearly as enthusiastically. Maxine must have been stunning as a young woman, but the years had not been kind to her. Too much sun and not enough care had taken their toll on her, though she was valiantly trying to disguise the fact with a rather liberal application of makeup. "I'm Maxine Halliday. And you are?"

Before I could speak, Jake answered for us. "We're the owners of the house you were snooping around this morning."

Instead of being intimidated by our knowledge, she simply laughed. "I'm afraid you'll have to be a little more specific than that. I'm often found creeping around places I don't belong. This morning I checked out four separate properties I'm going to try to get the listings for."

Jake gave her the address, and she nodded knowingly. "Oh, yes. I wanted a look at the place in person. The listing was gone nearly the moment it was placed, and I wanted to see if I'd missed something. I didn't," she said with that same ready smile. "You've got your work cut out for you on that project."

"That's an interesting hat you're wearing," I said, not able to help myself. It wasn't a part of the investigation, but I couldn't keep from staring at it, so I figured I had to say something about it or she'd notice my steady gaze at her covered forehead.

"It was a gift from a friend," she said, trying to blow my question off.

"That must have been some friend," I said softly.

I hadn't even realized that she'd heard me say it. "Why do you say that?"

"It's just that it's ... so flamboyant, wouldn't you say?" Flamboyant? Where had I come up with that?

"Thank you," she said, choosing to take it as a compliment. "Have you come by to ask me to represent you when you sell the property after you fix it up? You might be surprised to learn that you might make a larger profit if you sell it right now, as it stands. I've seen too many flips fail when people fail to account for all of the expenses they are going to incur."

"No, we want to do the remodel ourselves," Jake said, acting a bit offended by her assumption that he didn't know what he was doing.

"Suit yourself," she said. "Either way, it's always smart to line up the sales team first." Maxine pulled out an old-fashioned planner from an oversized handbag on the back of her chair and started flipping pages, frowning as she did so. "I'm really quite busy, but I may be able to fit you in. When is your projected finish date?"

"Eight weeks," Jake said.

"Really? How ambitious of you," she said as she started flipping more pages. "I can make that work." Maxine put the planner away and reached into one of her desk drawers, pulling out a thick sheaf of papers and sliding them across to us. "I just need you to sign this simple sales contract and we can get started."

"We have two other partners we need to consult first," I told her, trying my best to delay her from signing us up for something we didn't want. There was nothing simple about the contract she was offering, and I wouldn't sign it without Momma vetting it first, and then her attorneys.

"I see," she said a little coolly as she pulled the paperwork back toward her.

"We can take that with us," I offered as I reached for the contract.

The real estate agent was too quick for me, yanking it back toward her with a speed that was impressive. "Just bring everyone by, and we'll all sign the contract together at that point."

I had a hunch, and I decided to go with it. "Maxine, why do I get the feeling that you might already have a buyer interested in purchasing the house?"

"Why do you ask that?" she queried as she looked at me for a moment with open skepticism.

"Just curious, I guess."

Before the real estate agent could answer, her cell phone rang. "Sorry, but I've got to get this. Come back when you're ready to sign with me," Maxine added, and then she answered her phone call by saying, "One moment, please. I'll just be a second."

There was nothing more we could do, so Jake and I stood and started toward the door.

I wasn't ready to leave yet, though. I had a suspicion that I wanted to confirm if I could figure out a way to do it. That hat was still bothering me. The woman was stylishly dressed otherwise, but here she was, wearing the most garish monstrosity I'd ever seen, and to make matters worse, I was no fashion expert, but even I could see that it clashed with her outfit.

I turned and looked above her head curiously. "What's that?"

Maxine threw her head to the side quickly, and much to my delight, her hat tumbled down her back and landed on the floor. When it did, I saw that as she grabbed for it and jammed it back into place, there was a rather substantial bandage above the once-concealed eye.

Evidently the hat was meant to be something *more* than a fashion statement after all.

"My mistake. I thought I saw something, but I was wrong," I said quickly as Jake and I stepped outside before she could reply.

Once we were back out on the sidewalk, Jake said, "That was a nice move, Suzanne. How did you know?"

"It just didn't make any sense. The hat didn't match the outfit," I said.

"Or any outfit, if you ask me," he replied. "It appears she took a pretty solid blow if she needs a bandage that large."

"Maybe it's *not* related to the house," I said warily as we headed back to the truck.

"Suzanne, you don't believe that for a second, and neither do I. Maxine Halliday and Lionel Henderson both need to go on our list of suspects."

"Agreed, but do we honestly think that one of them had something to do with the counterfeiting and the break-in?"

"I don't know, but we're going to have to figure out a way to find out," Jake replied.

"How do you suggest we do that?"

"I say we head back to Henderson's office and see if he's still there."

"And if he is?" I asked.

"We park in front of his car so he can't get out of his parking space, and then we wait until he comes out. The man's got to go home sometime."

"What if he's already gone?"

"Then we go to his home. He shouldn't be that hard to find. Suzanne, there's something going on here that is more than meets the eye, and I intend to find out what it is."

"That's why you're such a good partner," I said as he drove back to Henderson's office. "You're like a dog with a bone when you're investigating a case."

"Funny, but that's exactly how I think of you," he said before realizing how it might sound to me. "Not that I'm calling you a dog. Far from it. I think you're beautiful."

I started laughing at his clumsy attempts to mollify me when I wasn't even all that upset with the comparison. "I *love* that we're both obsessed with uncovering the truth," I said. "There's no shame in that, at least in my book."

"Good," he said.

When we got back to Lionel Henderson's office, my worst fear was realized, though.

The luxury vehicle was gone, and so was the man himself, I was willing to wager.

"How do we find out where he lives?" I asked Jake.

"Let me check something," he said as he pulled out his cell phone.

"Are you calling an old buddy from law enforcement?" I asked him.

He just laughed. "No, at least not yet. I thought I'd look up his home address on the internet."

"Yeah, that makes more sense," I said with a smile.

After a few moments, Jake said, "I've got it. Let's go see if he headed home when he left here."

"I'm ready if you are," I said.

Henderson's home wasn't nearly as nice as I'd been expecting, given the man's attire and the vehicle he drove. In fact, I would say that it wasn't even as nice as the cottage that Jake and I shared. "Are you sure this is it?" I asked him.

"This is the address I found online, and we both know that the Internet doesn't lie." It was said with a sardonic grin, but really, what choice did we have?

Lionel Henderson answered the door, and he looked to be equal amounts of surprised and unhappy to find us once again on his doorstep. "What do you two want? I was under the impression that our business was concluded."

"There was bleach on your car door handle," Jake said, dispensing with all niceties. "What was worth getting rid of that is most likely going to ruin the finish on your car?"

"What are you talking about?" he asked with a frown. "I never put bleach on my car, the door handle or any other part of it."

"Would you like me to prove to you that *someone* did?" Jake asked as he gestured toward the car in question.

"How should I know who decided to vandalize my car? I run a business, not a charity, and sometimes the people I deal with forget that basic fact. I can't watch my vehicle the entire time I'm in my office. Unlike some people, *I* have work to do."

Was that a slam at Jake? I worked more hours than most people in the course of a week at Donut Hearts, but Jake was retired. Or at least he had been until he and Phillip had started on their house flip.

"I get that," Jake said, not backing down. "So, you're saying that you didn't do it?"

"Not that it's any of your business, but that's exactly what I'm saying," he replied.

"Then you wouldn't mind if I smelled your hands, would you?"

It was a brilliant move. I knew that bleach was a difficult smell to get off the skin, so if he'd accidentally splashed a little on his hands, we would probably still be able to smell it.

Henderson looked shocked by the request and immediately jammed his hands into his pockets. "I certainly do mind."

I saw a bit of movement toward the back of his house out of the corner of my eye, but by the time I looked, whoever had been there was gone.

"Sorry, we didn't mean to interrupt you. Who's your company?" I asked him.

This time his pause was more noticeable than it had ever been. "I can assure you that I'm completely alone."

"Sure, maybe you are now, but who just left? Would you mind if we came in and had a look around?" It was purely a hunch, but I wanted to see if there were any signs inside as to who his visitor might have been.

Evidently the request was too much for him to take. "That's it. I'm through with the two of you. Leave me alone. If you bother me again, I will call the police. What you are doing is harassment, pure and simple. My buyer was interested in the house, and now he's not. That is the end of my business with you. Now please leave, or I'm afraid I'll have to have you escorted off the property for trespassing."

Jake looked at me to see how I wanted to handle it, and after a moment, I just shrugged and turned away from Henderson. My husband followed me quickly, and Lionel Henderson remained silent until we were nearly back to the truck.

"I trust I won't be seeing either one of you again," he called out.

Jake and I didn't even break step as we got in and drove away. It was clear that we'd rattled the man, but had we done it with reason? Were things as he'd stated them, or was there something darker and more sinister lurking behind the scenes? Was it possible he was in fact working for a client, or was there a chance that he was the counterfeiter himself? Had that been *his* blood at the scene, or possibly even Maxine Halliday's? We hadn't really gotten any good answers during our investigation so far, just more and more questions, but that wasn't all that unusual, as frustrating as it might be.

There was only one thing we could do.

We had to keep digging until we turned something up that would lead us to whoever had been using our flip house for a counterfeiting operation, and whose blood it was that we had found at the house.

I wasn't sure what to do at the moment, and I hoped my husband had an idea we could pursue. After all, two heads had to be better than one, at least at the point we were at now.

## Chapter 13

"WHAT SHOULD WE DO NOW?" I asked Jake.

"I want to swing by the flip house," he said as he started driving.

"To talk to Agent Blaze?" I asked as innocently as I could.

"That too, but I'd also like to have a chat with Curtis Malone."

"Our neighbor? Do you think *he* might be involved in this?" I asked.

"I'm not saying that he is or isn't part of this. Look at it one way. If he is the one responsible for the counterfeiting, wouldn't it make sense for him to use our house for his base of operations instead of his own? After all, he's got easy access to the place, he can see who comes and goes, and he appeared to be as caught off guard by us buying the place as everyone else was. On the other hand, let's assume that he's clean. Given his proximity to the place, maybe he's seen something suspicious going on around the house while we've been gone. You've seen the man. He can't seem to keep himself from spying on us."

"Is it really spying, though? I thought he was just curious about what we're doing," I said.

"Maybe, but it just might work to our advantage if he's watching the place," Jake said.

As we drove by Curtis's home, I was surprised to see that no curtains flipped closed on our approach. In fact, there was no sign of the man at all. Maybe, with our temporary departure, he'd given up his vigilance.

There were two black sedans in the flip house's driveway, so it was clear that the Secret Service was still there.

I just wondered how much more they could actually do, given how bare the house was already.

I was about to find out.

"Agent Blaze, may we come in?" Jake asked formally as we both stood just outside the door.

"No, I'll join you out there," she said as she moved a wisp of red hair from her forehead. From the look of the place, they'd been busy.

"How's it going?" Jake asked.

"We aren't finished with our sweep yet, if that's what you're asking," she said.

I looked over her shoulder and saw that all of the light switches and fixtures had been pulled away from the walls and ceilings, and one agent was on his hands and knees tapping each and every floorboard, prying occasionally to see if any came loose, while another agent was probing at the ancient baseboard, covered with so many layers of paint that I had no idea how we were ever going to get them free. "It seems as though you're doing a thorough job," I said with a straight face.

"I missed something once. I'm not letting it happen again," she said resolutely. "I'm afraid it's going to be a few more days before you get your house back. We've just been working on the first floor, so we've still got the loft and the basement yet to examine."

"I get it," Jake said, though it was clear that he was as disappointed to hear the news as I was. I was eager for the project to get going again, and I couldn't even imagine how antsy Jake and Phillip must be to start working on the place once more. "Any chance it will be sooner than that?"

"No, I don't think so," she said firmly as her cell phone rang. One glance at the number, and she said, "I've got to take this. It's my direct supervisor."

Blaze stepped back into the house, but I was still hoping we might be able to overhear her side of the conversation when she shut the door.

"Wow, she's determined not to miss a thing this time, isn't she?" I asked Jake.

"She won't make that mistake again," he said. "If I know her, she's going to be here for at least another week looking for anything else she might have missed."

"Do you think there's anything left here for her to find?" I asked him.

"I'm not sure," he said after a moment's thought.

"Seriously? What else could there be?"

"I don't know, but whoever was here before clearly had some kind of physical confrontation. I'm guessing that shut down whatever they were going to do, so whatever they may have been trying to retrieve might still be here."

I didn't like the thought that there was something the bad guys still wanted with our flip house. I was tempted to open the doors and let them get whatever it was they so desperately wanted, but I knew that I was in the minority on that front. Agent Blaze, and to no lesser extent my husband, wanted the bad guy or guys brought to justice.

All I wanted was our house back.

Agent Blaze came out with a look of disgust on her face. "Here are your keys," she said as she handed them to Jake.

"I don't get it," I said. "What changed your mind?"

"Evidently there's a bigger problem on the coast with counterfeit hundreds that I need to investigate immediately. We'll be back when we wrap that up, but I've been given orders to turn the property back over to you in the meantime. As far as my immediate supervisor is concerned, this case goes on the back burner, especially since we have a suspect under arrest."

"But you don't believe Slick Willie did this any more than we do," I protested.

Blaze looked as though she were about to say something when she quickly changed her mind. "What I believe is of no consequence. I've been given my orders, and I mean to follow them." She softened a moment as she turned directly to Jake. "You understand, don't you?"

"Completely," he said. "Tell you what I'll do. As we work, I'll keep my eyes open for anything that might be of interest to you. We were planning on taking the walls down to the studs, so it's hard to imagine what we might find in our remodeling work. I'll document anything we find that might be of interest to you and let you know about it immediately."

"I'd appreciate that very much," she said, softening even more. "I always knew that I could count on you." She started to extend a hand to his shoulder when she glanced at me and changed direction to make it a handshake. "You've got my number."

"We both do," I said, offering my hand as well. Blaze took it briefly, and as she did, her staff came out of the house carrying a full set of tools between them.

"Let's move," she told them as they headed for their respective cars.

"Wow, can you believe that?" I asked Jake as I saw them drive away.

"Unfortunately, it's the way of the world these days. Law enforcement is so understaffed that there's not nearly enough time for old-fashioned police work anymore."

"You sound wistful for the good old days," I said gently. "Do you miss it too terribly much?"

He paused in thought for a moment before answering. "What I miss is having a purpose in life, but all in all, I wouldn't trade my time now with you for all of my tenure as a State Police inspector."

"I'm glad about that," I said as I turned back to the house. "Should we go in?"

"Yes, but I don't want to start work until morning since it's already getting dark. Who knows if the place even has power at this point?"

"I'd offer to flip the switch," I said as I looked at the dangling on/off switch hanging by three wires near the front door, pulled three inches away from the wall, "but it doesn't look safe."

"That's because it's not," he said. After we looked briefly around the first floor, Jake turned to me and frowned. "We really should get out of here. This place is a disaster area."

"You know what they say," I said, doing my best to reassure him. "You have to make it ugly before you can make it pretty again."

"Who says that?" Jake asked with a laugh as he dead-bolted the door behind us.

"You know, carpenters and remodelers and folks like that," I said.

"Well, as long as you've got concrete references to cite, how can I possibly disagree with you?" His smile faded as he pulled out his cell phone. "I need to tell your mother and Phillip what's going on here."

I touched his hand. "I have a better idea. Why don't we go tell them in person?"

Jake looked at me for a moment. "That doesn't have anything to do with the fact that it's nearly dinnertime, does it?"

"Why, Jake, what are you accusing me of?" I asked as innocently as I could manage.

"I'm not accusing, I'm congratulating you," Jake said. "I love your mother's cooking almost as much as I love yours."

"Now I know you're lying to me," I said with a grin. "Come on, let's go see if we can get another free meal. This is almost getting to be a habit with us, isn't it?"

"Maybe we'll take them out to dinner if your mother hasn't cooked anything," Jake offered.

"The thought is sweet, but if I know my momma, she's going to put out a big meal, even if it is just for the two of them."

"They must eat a lot of leftovers," Jake said as we got back into the truck.

"I'm certain of it, but her seconds are better than just about anybody else's firsts."

Jake pulled into Curtis's driveway instead of driving straight to Momma's, though. "We need to have a quick chat with him first, and then we'll be on our way."

The truth was that in all of the excitement about getting the house back, I'd forgotten about our decision to talk to our nosy neighbor. "Let me just give Momma a call and tell her we'll be stopping by soon."

"Don't tell her we got the house back yet," Jake said. "I want to tell them that in person."

"I won't," I said.

"Momma was thrilled we were coming," I reported a minute later, "but she couldn't quit apologizing that it was leftover night tonight, no matter how many times I told her we were excited about the prospect."

"She's your mother. What can I say?"

"What does that mean?" I asked him.

"Just that the apple doesn't fall far from the tree. You're more like her than you're willing to admit, Suzanne."

I shook my head. "I only wish that were true. She's a hard act to follow, you know?"

He took a moment and kissed me lightly. "I think you've cleared that particular bar with ease."

"That's sweet of you to say," I told him.

I looked up to find that the front door was opening even as we approached Curtis Malone's house, and from the frown he was exhibiting, it appeared that he wasn't happy to have his visits to our place reciprocated.

"Is there something I can do for you?" he asked us a little sternly as we got close. "I'm afraid I'm a little busy inside at the moment."

What had happened to the warm and friendly guy from the day before who'd brought Jake and Phillip cold beers? Evidently he wasn't nearly as big a fan of drop-ins at his place as he was of popping in on other people.

"We were just wondering if we could get your advice about something," Jake said. "Sorry to bother you right now. If it will help, we can come back tomorrow."

The change in him was sudden. Evidently Jake had chosen exactly the right way to approach him, by appealing to his vanity. "No, it's not that important. It can wait." He glanced back at the house and said softly, "I'd invite you in, but I'm in the middle of a project, and the place is a wreck." After a brief hesitation, Curtis added, "Though it's certainly not as big as the project you all have on your hands."

That got a chuckle from us, though it really hadn't been all that funny, but we wanted to get along with this man, at least for the purposes of this particular conversation. After all, who didn't like having someone laugh at their jokes, no matter how feeble they might really be?

"We understand completely," Jake said, and I nodded as well. "We were just wondering if you happened to see anything odd going on next door over the last three or four days."

"Do you mean even *before* you bought the place?" Curtis asked.

"It might help," Jake said.

"Do you know, those police officers at the house never even knocked on my door to ask me anything," he said. "They must have come by on one of my rare trips into town, because I found a business card for an Agent Blaze tucked behind my screen door with a handwritten message that she'd be in touch and that she wanted to get my fingerprints, but unless I'm mistaken, she and her team left not five minutes ago."

"You're right. They were suddenly called away," I said. "So, if they'd asked you about what you'd seen, what would you have told them?"

"Lots. You can trust me on that," he said smugly.

"Would you care to elaborate?" Jake asked him.

"I'd be happy to, if it would help. Okay, first of all, there was quite a bit of foot traffic going on over there for the past month."

"Not cars?" Jake asked.

"No. I'm not sure where they were parking, but I rarely saw any cars. There's a way to cut across the yards from the street next door without being seen. That's the way they must have come and gone."

"If you didn't see anyone drive past, how did you know anyone was there?" I asked him. "After all, you can't really see the place from here."

"Not so much in the daytime, but at night at this time of year, a light shines pretty clearly through the trees. I'm up a lot during the night, and on more than half a dozen occasions, I saw muted lights at night coming from a house that was supposedly empty. How can you explain that?"

I knew the reason, but I wasn't going to share it with the nosy homeowner. "It's a mystery," I said. "What else did you notice? Did you ever go over there for a closer look?"

He looked a little embarrassed. "Once. I just wanted to make sure that there was no hanky-panky going on, you know?"

"I understand completely," Jake said. "What did you see?"

"I only went over one time. That was plenty, believe me. I was getting close to one of the windows in front when the door suddenly opened! I nearly had a heart attack right then and there."

"Did they see you? And more importantly, did you see them?" Jake asked, his voice going into full investigative mode.

"No, I ducked back into the bushes before I could see who it was, but trust me, after coming so close to getting caught, I wasn't about to go over there again."

That was too bad, but I understood completely. Why should he take a chance like that merely to satisfy his own curiosity? Then again, I'd pushed my luck far past that on more than a few occasions, but I liked to think of myself as being outside the norm. Whether that was a good thing or a bad thing, I couldn't say.

"Did you happen to see anything more recently?" Jake asked him.

"Let's see. The day before you and your father-in-law showed up, a man drove down the road in a luxury car."

"Do you mean the day after?" I asked him, recalling the timeline of when Lionel Henderson III had come by the donut shop looking for me.

"Sure, he came by then too, but the first time he was there he stayed a lot longer. I thought it was odd at the time, but I didn't give it too much thought."

"Anything else?" Jake asked him.

"Just Maxine Halliday's car the next day," Curtis said.

"How did you know it was her?" I asked him.

"For one thing, her face is plastered all over every bus bench in town, but she also has a big magnet on the side of her car advertising her firm. She didn't stay long, about the same amount of time the man in the luxury car stayed the second time he was out here."

It was good to get outside confirmation about the presence of our suspects on our property. Then again, what if either one of them had been there not for the house but for what was inside of it?

"I'm afraid that's about all I've seen," he said. "I'd be more than happy to keep an eye on the place from now on if you'd like me to."

"That would be appreciated," Jake said.

I added quickly, "Just don't take any chances on our account though, okay?"

Jake shot me a curious look, but he didn't say anything.

"Of course," Curtis said. "Now if you'll excuse me, I've really got to get back to it inside."

"Thanks for speaking with us," Jake said. He reached into his wallet and pulled out a business card he'd had made when he'd first started freelancing. "If you see anything suspicious, give me a call anytime, day or night."

"I'll do that," Curtis said before disappearing back inside.

Once we were on the road back to April Springs and Momma's place, Jake asked me, "What was that all about?"

"What do you mean?"

"Curtis volunteered to be our eyes and ears on the ground, but you tried to discourage him."

"Jake, the man's a civilian and an amateur. Trust me, you don't want it on your conscience if anything happens to him because of us. I went down that road with George Morris before, remember?" The mayor, who hadn't been our mayor at the time, had nearly been run over by someone we'd been investigating together, and it was only recently that I could no longer see any signs of the limp that had once been so prominent in his walk.

"Suzanne, Curtis Mason is a grown man. If he wants to help us with surveillance at the property, passively of course, who are we to say no?"

"I won't say anything more about it," I said. "What do you think about what he told me?"

"I'd really love to speak with Henderson and Maxine Halliday again," Jake admitted. "Their stories don't quite add up, do they?"

"Well, we might get the chance to see them both tomorrow if you can fit some sleuthing into your construction schedule."

"That's true, we're going to be busy again very soon, but I just can't let this go."

"Do you mean like the Secret Service did?" I asked.

"You can't blame Blaze for that. I know what it's like to be countermanded by a superior. Believe me, it's no fun."

"So we'll keep our investigation up and running while you remodel the house and I run my business. It sounds like fun," I said with a brave smile.

"I know it's going to be a lot of work, but at least some of it will be part of what we're doing anyway. Trust me, if there's anything else to find in that house, Phillip and I will uncover it in the course of our remodel."

"Don't forget, Momma and I are going to help, too," I reminded him.

"Okay, I give up. You're going to have three jobs: donutmaker, re-modeler, and amateur sleuth. That's an awful lot on your plate, even for you."

"Don't worry about me. I can manage it," I said, though I wondered if I'd have any time left over for sleep in the course of the next several weeks. I had a feeling that if we didn't make any more progress on the counterfeit case, and if nothing else happened to pique our interest, it would fade into the background until we got more evidence as to who might have been doing it.

A part of me was afraid of that happening, but an equal part was just as happy that this case might never be solved.

After all, contrary to popular belief, I didn't have to investigate *everything* out of place that happened around me.

Then again, who was I kidding? I needed to know who had broken into our place, why there had been a scuffle, and who had been injured. I knew if I could answer those questions, I'd have a pretty good idea as to who the counterfeiter had been.

But until then, I had plenty to do.

Chapter 14

"DOT, THOSE MAY HAVE just been leftovers, but that meal still beat just about anything you can get out at the finest restaurant," Jake said as he pushed his plate away.

"Just about?" Phillip asked him. "Why the qualifier?"

"Phillip, you hush," Momma said. "They had lunch at Napoli's. I'm honored to be mentioned in the same breath as the DeAngelis family. How are they, by the way?"

"Just about perfect, at least as far as I'm concerned," I said. I studied my stepfather for a moment. There was something different about him, as though a dark cloud had descended upon him since I'd last seen him the day before. Had the troubles at the house gotten to him that much? Or was there something else going on? "Phillip, how are you doing?"

"I'm okay," he said, not making eye contact with me. "Why do you ask?"

"You just don't seem like your old self. Something seems to be troubling you," I said.

"Now that Suzanne's brought it up, I've noticed that you've both seemed subdued ever since we walked in the door. Is something going on?"

Momma looked at her husband and shrugged. He took a deep breath, moved some of the mashed potatoes around on his plate for a moment, and then said, "I got some test results back today."

"I didn't even know you had a test done," I said. "I'm guessing it wasn't good news."

"It wasn't," he said.

Momma patted his hand. "Phillip, it's going to be all right. We'll get through this, together."

"Now I'm really worried," I said. I'd grown quite fond of the man over the years. "Talk to us, Phillip. After all, we're family."

"It's your decision, dear," Momma said softly, reaching out and touching his hand lightly.

"I've got cancer," he said, and I felt my stomach drop.

"I'm so sorry. What kind do you have?" I asked him.

"So far it's just in my prostate, at least as far as they can tell. I won't know more until I have an MRI. At this point, I'll probably have to choose between surgery or radiation treatments. It's our call, and at the moment we're leaning toward the surgery, but we'll know more after the MRI." He looked at Jake. "When was the last time you had a physical?"

"It had to have been while I was still on the force," he admitted.

"Go get checked, and make sure they do a PSA test. Evidently it's not the greatest indicator of cancer in the world, and the biopsy's no fun if they find that your numbers are high, but it could save your life."

"How bad is it?" I asked him softly.

"Three of twelve areas tested showed cancer," he said matter-of-factly. "The good news, if you can call it that, is that they think they found it in time, unless it's spread. That's what the MRI is for. If it hasn't gone beyond my prostate, then after the surgery, there's a pretty decent chance I'll be fine."

"How are you feeling?" I asked him.

"If those results hadn't come back positive, I would have said I'm the perfect picture of health. That's the thing about this disease. From what I understand, by the time you get the first noticeable symptom, chances are that it's too late to do anything about it."

"Do you have any idea when you'll have the procedure?" Jake asked him.

"No, we haven't gotten to that point yet. Fortunately, I have some time to think about it, so it shouldn't interfere with our work on the flip, at least not right away."

Jake looked at him steadily before he spoke. "Phillip, that house should be the *least* of your worries right now."

"Jacob, we both feel that this will be the perfect diversion for us at the moment," Momma said. "The cancer is slow growing, so we have a little time before we need to do anything." She patted her husband's hand and smiled gently at him. "We'll get through this."

"You bet we will," Phillip said, trying to force a smile. I knew that he'd loved my mother nearly all of his life, but they hadn't been together for very long. Losing another husband would be traumatic for Momma, and if I was being honest about it, losing him would be tough on me, too.

"Okay. I get that. If there's anything we can do in the meantime, let us know, okay?" Jake offered.

"Just make that appointment," Phillip said.

"I'll make sure that he does," I told him.

Phillip clapped his hands down on the table. "Enough talk about doom and gloom. If it's all the same to you, I'd really rather not talk about it anymore. And do me a favor. Let's just keep this in the family. Okay?"

"Of course," I said as I reached out and squeezed his hand. I knew it wasn't much, but it was the best I could do.

"Is there anything you can tell us about the investigation so far?" Phillip asked us.

I glanced at Momma, who nodded her approval. If they wanted to get a little normalcy back into their lives for the moment, I was going to do everything in my power to help make that happen.

"As a matter of fact, we found out a few interesting things about two of our suspects," I said.

"Three of our suspects," Jake chimed in, correcting me.

"I still don't think Curtis Mason is a viable candidate for a counterfeiter," I said.

"I'm not saying he's my top choice, but he's been around an awful lot, sticking his nose into things. We have to consider the possibility that maybe he's more than just a nosy neighbor."

"Are you seriously considering Curtis?" Phillip asked. After a moment, he nodded. "Yes, I can see that. What if he's been putting on a friendly act solely to get close enough to find out what we're up to? It makes sense."

"Who are your other two suspects?" Momma asked.

"We're beginning to think that Lionel Henderson III may have had something to do with it. Momma, you said before that you knew him."

"I do, though not well," Momma said.

"Do you think there's a possibility that he's capable of being involved in this?" I asked her.

After a momentary pause, she said, "I have to say that I wouldn't put it past him."

"Who's your third suspect?" Phillip asked.

"It's a real estate agent named Maxine Halliday," I replied.

"I know her as well," Momma said gravely, surprising me with her admission, though I wasn't sure why. After all, my mother had her fingers in a great many pies in the area, quite a few of them dealing in real estate and investments.

"What do you think of her?" Jake asked her.

Momma mulled it over for a few moments before answering. "The truth of the matter is that either one of them could be involved in something illegal, and though I wouldn't have suspected them of being counterfeiters, it wouldn't surprise me, either. They are both too shady for me to work with, no matter how much they implore me to let them in on one of my deals. If that's what it takes to make money in this world, then I'd rather not do it."

"Why do you suspect them?" Phillip asked Jake.

"Mostly it's their mutual interest in the property. It seems a bit excessive to us," Jake said.

I expanded on that. "They've both been seen lurking around the flip house over the past several days, and we can't help wondering if their interests were more because of what was going on inside the house or because of the property itself. We've spoken to each of them, but we plan to talk to them both again tomorrow after we finish working on the house."

"I thought the Secret Service still had control of it," Momma said.

"Oh. We forgot to mention that, didn't we? Agent Blaze and her team were called away suddenly, and she turned the key back over to us," Jake replied.

Phillip smiled for the first time that day. "That's excellent news," he said heartily. "I can't wait to get my hands dirty again."

I was about to ask him if that was wise, given his condition, when Momma shook her head slightly. I'd seen that motion from her quite a bit over the years, so I shut down that line of questioning before it even got out of my mouth. "It sounds like fun to me, too," I said.

"Then it's settled. Bright and early tomorrow, we resume demolition," Jake said.

"I can't wait," Phillip answered when Jake's cell phone rang.

"I wonder what the police chief wants," Jake said as he glanced at his caller ID.

As the conversation developed, my husband's expression began to turn rather grim. "Hey, Chief. What's up? When? Okay. We're on our way."

Jake stood abruptly as he put his phone away.

"What's going on?" I asked him.

"There's a fire at our flip house," he said. "We need to go."

"I'll drive," Momma offered, and we all raced to her car so we could see just how much damage had been done.

I was beginning to feel as though the property the four of us had purchased actually *was* cursed, and as Momma raced to the scene, I had to wonder if the blaze had something to do with the counterfeiting or the inspection the Secret Service had conducted or if it was just a coincidence and not related to anything that had been going on there lately.

I hated coincidences though, and so did Jake.

No, I had to believe that this fire had to be directly related to what had happened over the course of the past few days.

What had they been trying to cover up, though?

It appeared now that we might never know.

Chapter 15

"WOW, THERE'S NOTHING left but cinders and rubble," I said as I looked at the shell of the place we'd been in earlier that day. Full-on night had fallen, but you'd never know it by the way the scene was lit up from the fire trucks and the police cruisers standing by, all beaming their lights on the burned remains of the house we'd owned so recently. "How did it burn down so fast?"

Smoke still wafted up from several hot spots, and the fire department dutifully treated the smoldering areas, but the place was clearly a total and complete loss.

"These older homes can be tinderboxes sometimes," Jake said. "I'm sorry I dragged you and Phillip into this, Dot. We don't have enough to make up for your loss, but Suzanne and I will pay you back every penny it took for you to buy it."

"Nonsense. I won't hear of it," Momma said.

"We insist," I replied.

"Suzanne, I love you and your husband for making the offer, but I had insurance on the place, so we'll be fine."

"What if it was burned down on purpose?" I asked gently. "Will you still get the money?"

"As long as I wasn't the one who set the fire, we'll still be all right," Momma said, "and I have three witnesses who can prove I was nowhere near this place this evening."

The fire chief, an older man named Harley Lane, walked over to us and took his helmet off. "I heard this was your place, folks. Sorry for your loss."

"Thank you, Chief. Any idea as to what started the fire?" Momma asked him.

"Officially? No, that might take a while for the paperwork to go through."

"And unofficially?" Momma asked him with a gentle smile. "After all, as you said, I have a vested interest in the place."

"It was an accelerant, no doubt about it. Based on the three gas cans we found burned up inside, whoever did it wasn't taking any chances."

At least that eliminated the Secret Service and their investigation. I'd been worried that there might have been a short in one of the switches, but I was no electrician, or fire chief either, for that matter.

"At least no one was in the house," Chief Lane said, and then he looked curiously at my mother. "Dot, please tell me that no one was in there."

"If they were, they were trespassing," my mother said as she stared at the volunteer fire department crew waving their hoses around and extinguishing the slightest bit of smoke. The smells were heavy and acrid, and I wasn't sure I'd ever be able to get the odor out of my clothes.

"Everything we can see looks good, but we're still trying to get into the basement," the chief said.

"Chief. Over here," a firefighter called out, and the fire chief excused himself.

"Who would do something like this on purpose?" Momma asked out loud. I wasn't sure if it was rhetorical or not, but even if it had been, it didn't stop Jake from answering.

"Whoever was using the place for their counterfeiting activities might have had a reason to burn it down."

"He's right, Dot. The fire has to be related to the counterfeiting," Phillip added.

"I'm just glad that no one was inside when it happened," I said, trying not to think about what might have been if Phillip and Jake had been trapped inside when the blaze had started.

"Hold that thought," Jake said grimly as he pointed to the chief, who was summoning Chief Grant over to him. "Something's going on."

I looked to where he was pointing and saw that the crew had begun in earnest to clear the debris from the steps leading into the basement. Stephen Grant tried to go down the stairs the moment they were cleared of debris, but he and the fire chief started having a heated argument about it. I could hear Chief Lane saying that it wasn't safe yet, but Chief Grant wasn't paying any attention. It wasn't that hard to eavesdrop on their conversation, because both men were clearly emotional about something.

"I have to see the crime scene for myself while there is still anything down there to see," the police chief said stubbornly.

"It's too dangerous," the fire chief answered.

"It doesn't matter," Chief Grant said. "Now you really need to let go of my arm. I'm thirty years younger than you are, and I'm in better shape, too."

"Do you think I couldn't stop you if I wanted to?" the fire chief asked him, suddenly lowering his voice. As Chief Lane finished speaking, six of his volunteers rallied around him, and I didn't like the odds against my friend.

Chief Grant took a deep breath, and then he said calmly, "I need two minutes, and then I'll come right back out. One of your men can go down there with me if you'd rather I didn't do it alone."

"I'm going with you," Chief Lane said.

There were several protests from his men, but he killed every last protest with a look that could catch concrete on fire. Chief Lane might be older than everyone else on the scene, *and* in the worst shape of the entire crew, but he was their leader, and there wasn't a single doubt in anyone's mind about that. When Chief Lane saw that his men were going to stand down and let him do as he'd promised, he turned back to Chief Grant. "Two minutes, and then we're coming right back up. You're on the clock right now."

As the men disappeared into the basement, I found myself holding my breath. These two chiefs weren't acting out of machismo or even some elevated opinion of their abilities. They were both just trying to do their jobs in the best way they could, and I found myself admiring both of them for their bravery.

I started counting from the moment they disappeared, and two seconds before I hit one hundred twenty, they came back up again.

We'd been watching idly by, but clearly the volunteer firemen hadn't. Two of them had retrieved a stretcher while the dual chiefs had been gone, and I had to wonder if they'd been expecting one or both of them to pass out while they'd been underground.

But the fire chief turned to his men as soon as they emerged and said, "Collect the body and then get out of there, pronto."

What? What body? "What's going on?" I asked Chief Grant as he rejoined us. "What did you find down there?"

"Unfortunately, the house wasn't empty when it burned down after all," Chief Grant said grimly. "They're pulling the body out right now."

"Were you able to identify who it was?" Jake asked.

"No, I'd never seen whoever it was before. It must have been the smoke that killed them, though."

"Why do you say that?" Momma asked him.

"There was no sign that the victim had been anywhere near the fire, and based on where we found the body, it would have taken quite a while for the fire to reach them."

"What if something else killed them and just left them there to burn?" I asked, not even realizing that I'd said it aloud. "That could have been the real reason for the fire, to hide the fact that whoever you found in the basement was murdered."

"What are you talking about, Suzanne?"

I couldn't shake the suspicion I was experiencing at the moment. "I have a feeling that when the coroner inspects your murder victim, the cause of death is going to be something not related to the fire that ended up killing them."

"So, you think this is related to the counterfeiting?" Chief Grant asked.

"It has to be, doesn't it?" Jake asked him. "Otherwise it's just too much to swallow. The real question is who is that body that they're carting off?" he added as he pointed to the firemen carrying the stretcher out of the basement and toward us.

"We might be able to help with the identification," I volunteered, despite the fact that my stomach was doing flip-flops at the mere thought of seeing another dead body.

"Thanks, but that's not necessary. We'll figure it out soon enough," the chief said, trying to mollify me.

"If I can help, I want to do it," I insisted.

To Stephen's credit, he didn't look at Momma, Jake, or Phillip; only me. "Are you sure you want to do this, Suzanne?"

"I'm positive," I said.

"Okay," he replied. Jake and Momma both looked at me inquisitively, but I just gave them my bravest smile.

The men stopped beside us once they reached us, and Chief Grant unzipped the black plastic body bag.

I'd already been expecting to see a familiar face, so it only took me an instant to identify the victim.

"That's Curtis Mason. He lives, or I guess I should say lived, right over there," I said, pointing to the edges of the man's house through the darkness.

## Chapter 16

"DO *any* of you have an explanation as to why he might have been in your house as it was burning down?" Chief Grant asked us.

"He must have been curious about what we were doing," Jake said.

When no one else spoke up, the chief said, "There's something you're not telling me. He's one of your counterfeiting suspects, right?"

"It's probably a reach, but we discussed the possibility," Phillip answered truthfully.

"That figures. Is that why you think he might have been skulking around inside? Do you think there's a chance that he started the fire himself to get rid of some evidence and he got himself trapped in the basement before he could get out?"

"You got down there okay with the house in ashes around you," I pointed out. "What makes you think Curtis couldn't have done the same thing?"

"If there were smoke and flames, he might have gotten disoriented," the fire chief said from behind us. "It happens more often than you might think."

"I don't know. I'm having a hard time buying it," I said.

"Suzanne, we really must leave this to the experts," Momma said. "They've dealt with these things more times than we can imagine."

"Of course I'm not discounting that," I said. "It just doesn't feel right to me. I was never all that serious about Curtis as a suspect, and I certainly never pegged him as an arsonist." I turned to Jake. "How about you?"

"At this point, I'm willing to believe that *anything* is possible," Jake said. "If you look at it one way, it does make sense. Suzanne, I've been in a few fires over the years, and what the chief said was on the money. When the smoke is billowing and the flames are racing, it's hard to tell up from down, let alone right from left."

"Maybe," I said with a shrug. "It's just kind of convenient, don't you think?" I asked him.

"What do you mean?" Momma asked.

"A suspect dies in the very fire that destroys the last bit of evidence," I said. "Everything is suddenly wrapped up in a nice neat package, if everybody goes along with the chief's theory."

"I never claimed that I knew that was what happened," Chief Grant said. "I just realize from experience that most of the time, the most obvious answer turns out to be the right one."

"I get what you're saying, but Suzanne still has a valid point," Phillip said. Was he coming to my defense, or did he actually believe what he was saying? I didn't care at the moment, because either way, it was really sweet of him.

"It's too soon to know anything until an autopsy has been performed," Chief Grant said.

"When do you think that will be?" Jake asked him.

"The coroner's kind of backed up at the moment, so it's probably going to take a few days," the police chief conceded. "We'll know more then."

"And in the meantime?" I asked him.

"I'd say you should all keep doing whatever it was you were doing before this happened, but that's going to be tough, isn't it? I'm sorry about your loss. Is there any chance you had insurance on the place?"

"I *never* sign paperwork for any real estate purchase without having insurance," Momma said. "It's been a sound policy all of my adult life, so while we won't profit from the purchase, we won't lose anything, either."

"Except the chance to make something broken whole again," Phillip said. I had to wonder if he was still talking about the flipped house, or himself. It had to be pretty traumatic hearing the news that he had cancer, and my heart went out to him and my mother. I hoped it all worked out in the end, but I knew they had a rough handful of months ahead of them even if everything worked out, and I didn't envy them any of it.

"Don't you worry," Momma said as she patted her husband's shoulder. "We'll come up with something else."

"I don't doubt it," he said. After he sighed for a moment, he added, "I'll be in the car if you need me."

After he was gone, Chief Grant asked, "Is he okay? That man was my boss since I first joined the force, and I can tell that something's going on with him."

I wasn't about to tell the police chief what was really going on, and evidently neither was anyone else. "He was counting on working on the flip house," Momma said by way of an explanation.

"There's plenty of time to find something else to do," Chief Grant said, trying to cheer Momma up.

It was exactly the wrong thing to say, since Phillip may have been running out of time even as we spoke, but if it bothered my mother, she was too gracious to acknowledge it.

"Thank you for your kind words," she said. "I understand we have no right to learn the truth about the official cause of that man's death, but he passed away in our house, and I'd honestly like to know what happened to him."

"Like the fire chief said, it was probably smoke inhalation, but I'll let you or someone in your family know as soon as I do," Chief Grant said.

"I would greatly appreciate that," Momma replied before turning to us and heading for her car.

As we started to walk, Chief Grant asked, "Jake, do you have a second?"

"Sure," he said. "We all do." He was clearly saying that if the police chief wanted his opinion about something, he was going to have to take the rest of us as a package deal as well.

To his credit, Chief Grant agreed quickly. As he did so, the fire chief said, "If you'll excuse me, I've got to get back to my men. Sorry again for your loss, ma'am," he said to my mother.

"It's appreciated," she said.

Once he was gone, the police chief asked, "Who else is on that list of suspects besides Curtis Mason?"

Jake looked at me. "Suzanne, you should tell him. You've got a better handle on this than I do."

That was patently false, but I appreciated the gesture. "We have two other people we are considering," I said. "One is Maxine Halliday, and the other is Lionel Henderson III."

He looked surprised to hear the names. "Mind telling me why you think they might be involved?"

"They were both seen multiple times around the house, and they both have expressed what feels to us to be an inordinate amount of interest in a run-down old shack." I turned to Jake and added, "No offense."

"None taken. We hadn't even really gotten started yet," he said.

Chief Grant nodded. "Do you agree with that assessment, Jake?"

"One hundred percent," he answered.

To my surprise, the police chief then looked at my mother. "Mrs. Hart? What are your thoughts on the matter?"

"It's Dorothy, or Dot, as I've told you a dozen times," Momma said. "Yes, I agree with Jake and Suzanne."

"Well, I'll start doing some digging and see what I can uncover," he said.

"Are you going to call Agent Blaze?" I asked him.

Chief Grant looked a little guilty as he admitted, "As a matter of fact, that was going to be my next call. After all, she has a right to know."

I couldn't disagree with that, even though I'd found myself hoping that the Secret Service agent would make herself scarce for at least a little longer.

"It's the right thing to do," Jake said.

Momma sensed a lull in the conversation and said, "Well, there is clearly nothing else we can do here. Let's head back to town, you two. Suzanne, I know it's getting late for you."

"I'm not sleepy," I said even as I stifled a yawn.

"Of course not, but you owe it to yourself to at least try to get some rest. Come on, you two, I'll drive you back to my place, and you can pick up Jake's truck and head back to the cottage."

I was about to protest when I realized that I was exhausted. Heading back home was exactly what I needed.

We didn't talk much at all on the drive back to Momma's house, and after briefly saying our good nights, I gave my stepfather an extra-long hug. "Hang in there, you hear me?"

"I'm not going anywhere if I can help it," he said softly.

When I pulled away from him though, I could see, for one fleeting instant, a hint of concern in his eyes. I couldn't really blame him. Anytime the word "cancer" was mentioned, it was scary stuff.

I would do anything in my power to buoy his spirits, but for now, I had to get home and get some sleep.

The second we were alone, I turned to Jake as he started the short drive back to our cottage. "Did you mean what you said earlier?"

"I usually try to, but you'll have to be a little more specific than that," he told me.

"Is it possible that Curtis was the counterfeiter, and that he died when he tried to burn down the house and destroy any evidence he might have left behind?"

Jake tapped the steering wheel idly for a moment before he spoke. "I don't know, Suzanne. I know it *feels* convenient, but you didn't see how eager he was every time he came over to the house. I can't help but think that he was checking to see if we'd discovered something he didn't want found. If he wasn't the counterfeiter, why would he do that?"

"He was a lonely old man, and you and Phillip represented a big adventure to him. Why *wouldn't* he make a nuisance of himself and want to know what was going on every step of the way?"

I saw Jake glance in my direction and grin. "Is that what I've become since I left the State Police?"

"No," I said, but after a moment I added, "Not completely, at any rate. I'm so sorry about the house. I know you had your heart set on flipping it with Phillip."

Jake paused again, and it surprised me how carefully he seemed to be choosing his words. "In the end, maybe it's for the best."

That was surprising to hear, to say the least. "You don't mean that, Jake. You were so excited about it a few days ago."

"The truth is, I'm not getting any younger, Suzanne," Jake said. "I spent one morning working on the house, and I feel as though I went three rounds in the ring today. I may not be cut out for that kind of hard labor anymore."

That was so unlike my husband that I had to look hard at him to see if I could tell what was really bothering him. "Is it Phillip's condition that's got you so down?"

"Suzanne, you heard the man. He felt fine. The next thing he knew, he had cancer, and now he and your mother are making some very hard choices. I just keep wondering how I'd react if I got that kind of news."

"Jake Bishop, you're at least fifteen years younger than he is, and you're in better shape than any man your age has a right to be. You shouldn't let this worry you."

"How can I not?" he asked. Jake reached out and patted my hand. "It's given me a chance to think about what's really important to me."

"And have you come to any conclusions?" I asked as we passed Donut Hearts. We'd be home soon, and I knew that as soon as we finished driving, it would be much harder to discuss what was on my husband's mind. There was something about being in a vehicle that allowed us to speak more freely than if we were sitting across from each other on our couch, or anywhere else, for that matter.

"I need to work," he said, "and not hard labor. I want to figure out a way to use my skills that came so hard to me."

I tried to bury any panic I was feeling when I thought about Jake rejoining the police in any capacity. I knew that it was selfish of me to worry about him, but I'd never slept better than when he'd been officially retired from law enforcement, and I wasn't sure I could take it if he went back. "Are you going to try to be a state police investigator again?"

"What? No. The truth is that I'm not sure what I'm going to do. I just wanted you to know what I was thinking about."

"I appreciate that, and you know I'll support you in any way that I can," I said. I felt as though I'd just gotten a reprieve, though I didn't know how long it might be good for. "We don't have to figure it all out tonight," I added. "Let's go in, and I'll make us both some hot chocolate."

"Thanks. That sounds great. Are you sure you don't want to go straight to bed?"

"I can spare twenty minutes for my best fella," I said with a smile.

"Your *only* fella, you mean," he asked me with a grin nearly as big as mine had been.

"My one and only," I said.

Chapter 17

AS I DROVE BRIEFLY the next morning through the darkness to Donut Hearts, I was happy that I had somewhere to go, a place that I belonged. I knew that Jake had been missing that for some time, and if he could find something, anything, that would give him satisfaction and purpose again, I was all for it, even if it meant that he was going to be away from me for long stretches of time again. When it came right down to it, his happiness was more important to me than mine. After all, wasn't that what marriage should be, at least in a perfect world? My world was far from perfect, but having Jake in my life certainly made it immeasurably better.

To my surprise, there were already lights on in the donut shop as I parked my Jeep. When I looked inside, I saw Emma sitting at one of the tables, but the fact that she was there early was fine with me.

It was the person sitting across from her that disturbed me.

Evidently Ray Blake was not finished questioning me about the flip house.

"Ray, what are you doing here?" I asked coolly as I walked in and locked the door behind me.

"Suzanne, I wanted to get your permission first, but Dad insisted," Emma explained, trying her best to defuse the situation.

"I can speak for myself, young lady," Ray said. "I'm here to talk about Curtis Mason."

I turned on my heels and walked straight back to the door. After unlocking it, I held it open and turned back to Emma's father. "Goodbye, Ray."

He didn't budge from his seat, though. "Suzanne, the people of April Springs have a right to know."

It was a tired old line that he'd tried on me many times before, but I wasn't going to fall for it now, just as I hadn't any other time he'd tried to use it on me. "I'm not going to tell you twice."

Emma stood and pulled on her father's arm. "Dad, I told you this was a bad idea. Come on. You've got to go."

"What's she going to do, Emma, call the police on your own father?"

I pulled out my cell phone. "What a great idea. This is your final warning. If you're not out of here in thirty seconds, I'm going to have you physically removed. You're on private property, and you're not welcome here."

"I have every right to be here. I'm with my daughter," he protested.

I thought it was low of him to bring Emma into it, but evidently she thought even less of it. "You need to go like Suzanne said, or I'll call Mom, and we both know that's much worse than anything the police can do to you."

That got Ray's attention. "You wouldn't dare."

"Try me," Emma said as she stared hard at him.

He quickly got up and left without looking at me twice. Emma's threat had clearly been more incentive for him to leave than mine had been.

"I'm so sorry," Emma tried to explain.

"I am, too. You need to go home, Emma."

My assistant and dear friend looked stricken by my instruction. "Suzanne, you're *firing* me?" she asked, whimpering softly after saying it.

"No, but I need a little time to be alone."

"Suzanne, I said I was sorry," she tried again.

"It doesn't matter how sorry you are, at least not at the moment. Emma, you know how I feel about this place. It's my sanctuary, and your father invaded it, with your help, no less." They were hard words, but they had to be said. I wasn't getting rid of her for good, but if she chose to quit, it would be her own decision. I loved Emma like a daughter, but this time she'd gone too far.

She got up obediently and headed for the door, but before she left, she turned back and looked at me so sadly that I nearly caved in, but I held my resolve. "May I at least come back to work tomorrow?"

"That would be fine. I'll see you then," I said, smiling for the briefest of moments.

The relief that swept over her was clear, but she saddened again when I locked the door behind her and went back to the kitchen without even one glance back.

It appeared that I'd be spending the day alone at the donut shop, but that was okay with me. I'd done it for years, for at least once a week for as long as I'd had the place. I just hoped that Emma learned her lesson, and from the expression on her face, I had a feeling that she had gotten the point.

There was a Zen-like state to the rhythm of making donuts alone, and though I knew I'd have to stay late to finish up the dishes and do the other chores that Emma normally performed every day, it was necessary. I tried to put all of that out of my mind and focus on making the cake donut batter. After I had the basic recipe, I divided the dough into eight different bowls and started mixing up the individual flavors I'd be offering that day. I usually held one of the smaller batches out to experiment with, but at the moment there was nothing I really felt like trying, so I made a double batch of sour cream donuts, since that was by far my best-selling cake donut. The oil was ready by the time I'd finished mixing the last batch, so I got to work frying donuts, washing the dropper between batters so one batch wouldn't be tainted by the flavor combinations of the one before it.

Once the cake donuts were fried, iced, and put on trays, I started gathering the ingredients for my yeast donuts. After the dough was mixed and ready for its first proof, I debated on whether to take my usual break outside or just get started on the mound of dirty bowls and utensils I'd created. I even went so far as to start running the hot water, but I shut it off almost immediately. The work would be there for me later, but right now, I needed a break.

Grabbing and setting my timer, I headed for the front, only to find Ray Blake standing outside. I was going to turn around and go straight back into the kitchen, but when I saw the flowers in one hand and the sign in the other, I relented. Besides a cluster of daisies, one of my favorites, Ray had made a sign that said, I'M SORRY. That combination, as well as the hangdog look on his face, was enough to buy him at least two minutes of my time.

"What can I do for you, Ray? I'm not going to talk about what happened at the house last night, so if that's why you're here, you're wasting your time."

"I'm not here about the story. Emma told me what happened."

"Let me guess," I said as I refused the flowers he continued to offer. "She asked you to apologize for her."

The newspaperman looked genuinely shocked by the thought. "If Emma knew what I was up to, she'd be even angrier with me than she already is."

"Ray, you should have known better, and Emma should have, too. I can't have you invading my personal space," I told him.

"I get that, but don't punish her for my mistake. I didn't give her much choice."

"You didn't hold a gun to her head, did you?" I asked him.

"What? Of course not, but she knew it was a bad decision, and in her defense, she tried to warn me that it might go bad," Ray said.

"Then why did you push her into doing it?"

"I lost my head. That story, at least for that moment, became the only thing that mattered to me."

"And now?" I asked him.

"I've come to my senses. Emma and Sharon are truly all that I care about. Everything else in my life ties for last."

Ray seemed to be truly sincere, at least as far as I could tell. I took the flowers, and to his surprise, the sign as well. "Don't ever do that again," I said.

"I won't. I promise. Can Emma come back to work now?"

I was tempted, especially given the stack of things that needed to be washed waiting for me, but I couldn't do it. "No. But you can tell her I'll see her tomorrow."

"Okay. I get that. Thanks."

"I'm not doing it for you, Ray," I said a little coolly.

"I understand completely," he said. As he started to leave, he said, "Suzanne, I'm thrilled you took the flowers, but I'm curious about one thing."

"You want to know why I took the sign, don't you?" I asked him.

"Exactly."

"I'm putting it up in the kitchen as a reminder to Emma that Donut Hearts is a special place that deserves to be treated as such."

He merely nodded, and then the newspaper editor slunk away into the dark night.

I had three more minutes on my break when he left, and I wasn't about to squander them. I sat at one of the outdoor chairs we had for our al fresco diners and took a few deep breaths. No matter what time of year it was, there was something magical about the hours between midnight and sunup. It was almost as though the world was a different place, full of its own pleasures and secrets.

By the time my timer went off, I was ready for the next phase of my donutmaking operation, and I planned on getting every last ounce of joy out of it that I could.

When I went into the dining area to open the front at precisely six a.m., I found an angry woman waiting just outside the door, obviously chomping at the bit, wanting to get in.

"Maxine, are you here for donuts?" I asked her with a forced smile as I let her inside.

"I wouldn't eat one of those things if you paid me," she said angrily. "I don't know what you thought you were doing, but you're going to pay for it."

"I don't know what you're talking about," I said, which was technically true, which was a nice change of pace for me.

"The police came to my home last night and asked me some of the same questions you and your husband did yesterday afternoon. Did you tell them I was responsible for running some kind of counterfeiting ring?"

"No, I never said that," I said. While it was literally true, I had certainly implied it, but I wasn't about to admit it to this angry woman. "What did you tell them?"

"That it was ridiculous on the face of it! I run a successful realty company. Why on earth would I risk that for something so illegal, not to mention dangerous?"

"How is counterfeiting dangerous?" I asked, backing a few steps away. I could almost feel the heat coming off her, she was so angry.

"I consider prison a dangerous place, don't you?" Maxine asked me snarkily.

"If you didn't do anything, then you don't have anything to fear," I replied.

"Oh, grow up, Suzanne. In the world we live in today, the mere implication that I committed a crime is as bad as a confession in most people's minds. You're ruining my business, and I'm not going to stand for it. You'll be hearing from my attorneys before the day is through."

"What could you possibly sue me for?" I asked her. I'd led dozens of investigations in the past, but I couldn't remember anyone ever threatening me with a lawsuit because of it before, though it was entirely possible that it had happened and it had just slipped my mind. I'd been involved in far too many murder investigations in the past to keep track of every single threat that had been leveled at me.

"Let's see, there's defamation of character and loss of livelihood, and that's just the start. Once my attorney gets through with you, you'll be lucky to be able to afford to *buy* a donut, let alone run a stand like this."

"It's a full shop, and I doubt you'll be able to make anything stick. I'm sure my mother's attorneys can shut yours down."

She sneered at me. "Aren't you a spoiled little girl, running to your mommy when the mean lady threatens you."

"You'd better believe I am," I said. "Now, if you're not here to buy anything, I have customers waiting outside."

It was true, too. Three of my regulars were standing outside, no doubt afraid to come in given the volume of Maxine's threats.

"You haven't heard the last of this," she said as she turned toward the door.

I decided that while I had her there, I might as well ask her something, though I doubted there was one chance in a thousand that she'd actually answer my question. "Maxine, I'm curious about something. Where were you between the hours of six and seven p.m. last night?"

Maxine whirled around and faced me. "I had to tell the police, but I'm under no obligation to say anything to you. Go bark at the moon, donut lady."

Once Maxine was gone, George Morris, our mayor and one of the folks standing outside waiting to get in, came in and asked, "What was that all about? Please tell me that wasn't just another satisfied customer."

"What can I say? The lady was a little upset that I didn't have any pumpkin donuts on the menu today," I told him.

"Sure, that's all it was." George took a step closer. "Suzanne, are you okay?"

"Right as rain, besides the fact that our flip house burned down last night, with someone in the basement at the time."

"I heard," George said. "I'm sure the chief will get to the bottom of it soon enough."

"The police chief or the fire chief?" I asked him.

"Harley's a good fire chief, but he's no detective," George said. "I'm talking about Chief Grant."

"I know he's good," I said.

"Does that mean that *you're* not going to dig into what happened?" the mayor asked me.

"What do you think, George?" I asked.

"I think it's a silly question. Well, if there's anything I can do, just say the word."

"What can I get you today, Mr. Mayor?" I asked, desperate to change the subject.

"I'll take a dozen sour cream donuts and a cup of coffee," he said.

"Do you want to eat them here, or is your order to go?" I asked him with a grin.

"Funny, Suzanne. The council's not happy with me for keeping them waiting yesterday, and I'm trying to push something through one of the council's infernal committees, so I thought I'd soften them up with some of your treats first."

"My guess is that you're going to need more than these," I said as I boxed up the requested treats.

"We'll see. Never underestimate the power of the donut," George said with a broad smile.

"I haven't yet," I said. I put an extra donut in the box, got him some coffee, and made change from the twenty-dollar bill he'd offered me. "Is that it?"

"For now," the mayor said. "Keep me posted, okay?"

"I'll do my best, but it might take me a while to get back to you."

"I don't mind that. Just don't forget me," George said.

"I don't see how that's even possible," I replied. I was more upset about the confrontation with Maxine than I let on. I knew Momma's lawyers were powerful, so I tried not to let that part of it worry me, but I hated the idea of having my name associated with what she was about to accuse me of. I'd ask Momma about it later, but for now, it was time to sell the treats I'd worked so hard to create, something I loved to do.

If Maxine decided to pursue a lawsuit against me, I had a feeling I'd be able to weather the storm. Maybe her threats were good news. If she thought we were getting close, the real estate agent might believe that threatening me with legal action would get me to back down.

How little she knew me.

If anything, it made me even more resolved to find the person who had killed Curtis Mason, because there was no way I believed he'd died starting that fire, no matter how it might have looked to the rest of the world.

## Chapter 18

"MOMMA, I'M SO GLAD to see you," I said when my mother walked into Donut Hearts a little after nine. "As a matter of fact, I was just getting ready to call you."

"What a coincidence. I have two things to discuss with you myself. First of all, now that the flip house is gone, we need to come up with something to occupy our husbands." She paused for a moment before adding, "Something productive, I mean. They were so excited about the project that I feel we need to find another one for them."

"I'm not sure Jake is interested," I said, relaying our conversation from the night before.

"That's too bad," Momma said. "Was that why you wanted to speak with me?"

"No, it's about something else entirely. Maxine Halliday came into the shop first thing this morning and started threatening me."

My mother's maternal instincts kicked in at once. Her gaze narrowed and her voice hardened as she said, "Tell me what happened."

"She said she was going to sue me for giving her name to the police. Maxine said I was going to get hit with two or three lawsuits before the day was over."

"That's complete and utter nonsense," Momma said. "Give me two minutes, Suzanne." She looked around the donut shop and saw that several people were trying to pretend not to be listening in on our conversation and failing pretty miserably at it. "May I use your kitchen?"

"By all means," I said.

I was sure that it wasn't my imagination when I saw several disappointed faces. That was just too bad. Enough of my life was on display running the donut shop in the normal course of events. I had no desire to share any of the rest of it with the world. I couldn't understand why some people felt the compulsion to broadcast every thought that ever raced through their heads to the rest of the world, let alone every bite they took or every time anything of even vague significance happened to them. I knew I was in the minority feeling that way, but that was okay with me. When it came right down to it, I was just a simple donut-maker who liked to live her own life without being under the scrutiny of the ever-narrowing focus of the rest of the world.

Momma came out a bit more than two minutes later, not that I was watching the clock. Who was I kidding? I had stared at it so hard I was surprised it didn't break from the intensity of my attention. After all, we were talking about my future here. A lawsuit, no matter how friv-olous it might be, would wipe me out in legal fees alone, and that was even if I won. "What did you find out?" I asked her.

"Don't worry about a lawsuit. It's been taken care of."

"What did you do, Momma?"

"I made it go away. Isn't that enough?" she asked a little smugly.

"I'm afraid I'm going to need more than that," I said.

"I spoke with Maxine and reminded her of a few things, so she gra-ciously decided not to pursue it. Is that enough?"

"I'm not sure," I said.

"You don't seem that pleased. Isn't that the outcome you were hop-ing for?" Momma clearly looked confused by my reserved reaction to her news.

"It's not that. I'm grateful as always. I just don't want you doing any-thing you're not comfortable with doing on my behalf."

"Suzanne, my dear, never underestimate the power of a mother hen protecting one of her chicks," Momma said with a gentle smile.

"You must have some kind of clout with the woman. She seemed so determined when she was here earlier."

"If you must know, I reminded her of a few deals she made in the past that were a little more than merely ethical violations," Momma said.

"How did you know about them?" I asked, honestly curious about my mother's underground news network.

"I've been in the business of buying and selling real estate in this area for a very long time. Secrets can't help but find their way to me, and what I don't hear about directly, I am able to discover without a great deal of effort. That brings me to the second reason for my visit."

"What's going on?"

"I have news about both Lionel Henderson III and Maxine Halliday. Which would you like to hear first?"

"Hang on a second," I said. "Does anyone need a refill, or anything else?" I asked my customers.

When everyone there shook their heads, I turned to Momma. "Let's step into the kitchen."

"But what if a customer comes in?"

"I can prop the kitchen door open. If I'm needed up front, I'll know it."

Momma agreed, so we walked back into the kitchen together. From experience, I knew that I could block the door so that I could see the front door as well as the register. It wasn't perfect, since I liked to let the world know that I was there and ready for anyone who might need anything, but it would have to do, at least for the moment.

"Okay, I figure we have two or three minutes before I have to go back up front," I said. "Can I get the short versions of what you were able to find out about each of them?"

"Of course," Momma said. "First of all, Lionel Henderson is in some pretty deep financial trouble. He overextended himself at exactly the wrong time, and if he doesn't come up with a substantial amount of money in the next eight days, he's going to lose everything he owns, including the shirt on his back. He's desperate for money, and several folks in the real estate business know it."

"Then he could have turned to counterfeiting to try to bail himself out," I said. "That's certainly worth looking into. What else have you got?"

"Maxine opened her new office space assuming the market would continue to go up, but as everyone now knows, it's gone stagnant at the moment. She, too, needs money. I think that was the reason she threatened you with a lawsuit. She hoped you would settle to make it go away and help pay her rent for the next few months. The fact that she chose to go after you, knowing that I would do whatever it took to defend you, shows just how desperate she is."

"So, both of our remaining suspects have plenty of motive to try to create some sudden income," I said. "The next question is, which one of them had the ability?"

"I'm afraid that's not the question at all," Momma said, gently correcting me. "With the advent of color laser printers, reproduction isn't the difficult part. It's the paper that's impossible to find. Discover which one of them has access to that, and you're on your way to finding Curtis Mason's killer."

"Do you believe he was murdered, too?" I asked her.

"Suzanne, I've never lost anything betting on your instincts. If you feel so strongly about it, then I can't believe otherwise unless I'm faced with overwhelming evidence to the contrary. The next question is what are we going to do about it?"

"Jake and I need to do a little digging after I close the shop," I said.

"What should Phillip and I do in the meantime?"

I didn't know how to put it delicately, so I chose to be more direct than I would have liked. "Momma, if all four of us show up on someone's doorstep, there's no way they are going to tell us anything. You need to trust Jake and me and let us handle it."

She protested. "You seem to keep forgetting that Phillip is a trained law enforcement officer, too."

"I don't, so anytime you want to, you can stop reminding me," I said, doing my best to mollify her. "But Jake has experience well beyond that of any sheriff or police chief. I'm basically just tagging along with him on these investigations."

"Don't sell yourself short, young lady. Your contributions are always crucial to solving the cases you investigate, and you know it. False modesty doesn't become you."

"Okay, I'm a whiz-bang detective too, just not in the way that Jake is," I admitted with a smile.

"That's why it's so important that you have each other." She looked around and said, "My, but those are a great many dirty dishes."

"I'm working alone today," I told her, not getting into my reasons for sending Emma home. It was a family matter, not between my mother and me, but between my assistant and me. There was no need to air our dirty laundry in front of anyone else.

"I have an idea. What if Phillip and I come by when you are closing and clean the shop for you? It will free up your time and give us something productive to do as well."

I touched her arm lightly. "Momma, as much as I appreciate the offer, you don't know where anything goes, and I'm pretty particular about my kitchen. I can't even tell you how long it took me to teach Emma where I liked everything to be stored."

"I have no doubt about that," she said. "Isn't there *anything* we can do?"

"I'll tell you what. If we're able to run anything down, we'll bring you in to help. You don't need to stay on high alert or anything, but just knowing that you're there will be a comfort to both of us." I knew that it wasn't much, but it was the best I could do, given the circumstances.

"Very well," Momma said, doing her utmost to put on a brave face. "We'll await your call."

There was something about the glimmer in my mother's eyes that made me ask, "Momma, you two aren't going to go rogue on us and investigate without us, are you?"

"Suzanne, where on earth do you ever get these ideas?" she asked, feigning hurt feelings.

I knew her too well to let it go at that. "You didn't answer me. I want you to swear to me right here and now that you're not going to do anything without running it by Jake and me first. Promise me, Momma."

She was about to say something when the front door chimed, and I saw that I had a pair of new customers.

"You'd better take care of them."

My mother appeared to be just a little too smug about it. I didn't move a muscle as I said, "Not until you promise me."

"They may get tired of waiting and just leave," Momma pointed out.

"That's all on you then, isn't it? I've got all the time in the world."

One of the men who'd come in kept looking around, and finally he asked one of my other customers, "Is this place even open?"

"Suzanne," Momma said curtly.

"Momma," I replied, not moving an inch.

One of the men turned to the other one. "Come on, Joe. It looks like nobody's home."

"Very well. I promise," Momma said quickly.

"Thank you," I told her, and then I hurried out front. I really hated the idea of losing two customers, but my mother's pledge had been more important to me than even that. "Excuse the delay, gentlemen. I had to take care of something in back."

"That's okay," one of them said as he kept heading toward the door. "We don't have time to wait."

"How about if I throw in a few free donut holes for your trouble?" I asked.

"Come on, Joe, we're not in that big a hurry," the other one said to his impatient companion.

"I guess not," Joe said.

After I filled their orders and threw in the free treats, an older regular customer of mine named Travis approached. "I had to wait for my next donut order, too. What do I get for free?"

"Travis, you've been coming here for years, and your order is always the same: one small coffee and one bear claw. Are you trying to tell me that it's a coincidence that you suddenly want something else, too, the second you heard me giving away donut holes?"

"What can I say?" he asked with a grin. "Those donut holes look even better when they're free."

I had to laugh at his response. "I can't argue with that." I glanced at the clock and saw that my main rush was over. At times I'd thought about closing the shop at ten instead of eleven, so if today was typical at all, I'd end up having more leftovers than I liked. Grabbing a plastic glove, I put two donut holes on a napkin and shoved them across the counter to Travis.

He took them with a broad smile. "Thank you kindly, ma'am. Don't you want my extra order, too?"

"Did you really want anything besides those holes?" I asked him with a smile.

"Not really," he admitted, "but a promise is a promise."

"Don't worry, you're off the hook." I turned to the rest of the crowd. "Anybody else care for a few free donut holes?"

Every hand in the shop went up. After I gave everyone a pair of holes, I came back to find Momma smiling at me. "That was smart of you."

"What, giving away my treats instead of selling them? I didn't think you'd approve."

"On the contrary, I think you do a marvelous job here," she said. I loved it when she praised me, especially when it was unconditional.

"Those holes are simply scraps from the donutmaking process, aren't they?"

"Yes. I don't charge much for them, and they're a good way for my customers to try out different flavors without committing to an entire donut."

"See? I told you that you were smart. They taste a hole and then they buy a donut, or I imagine at least most of them do, I wager."

"I hate to turn down any praise that I can get, but the truth is that I didn't do it from a marketing standpoint. I just thought it would be a nice thing to do. Sometimes I like to do things with no obvious gain for me. If it makes me happy, and sharing my treats definitely qualifies, then I do it without giving it too much thought."

"You have a kind heart, Suzanne."

"What can I say? I got it from my parents," I answered.

Momma's eyes teared up a bit, and as she dabbed at the corners with a linen handkerchief, she said, "I'm afraid allergy season is upon us in full force."

"That must be it," I said. "If you're heading home, why don't you take Phillip a few treats? It might pick his spirits up."

"If your confections ever fail to do that, that's when I know that he's in serious trouble," Momma agreed.

I bagged up a nice assortment for him, and when I turned back to hand them to my mother, I saw her hand instinctively go for her purse. With my brightest fake smile, I said, "Momma, if you try to pay me for doing something nice, you and I are going to have a real problem."

Her hand pulled back immediately. "I was going to do nothing of the sort."

I grinned at the obvious lie, and I was happy to see that Momma's smile was nearly as broad as mine.

"We'll be in touch," I said as I kissed her cheek.

"I look forward to it," Momma said as she returned the gesture. I could tell that Phillip's cancer was weighing on her, and honestly, how could it not? But for at least a moment or two, I'd made her smile, and that was something I could be proud of. My mother was the toughest, smartest, bravest woman I knew, but that didn't mean that she couldn't be worried or scared sometimes too, especially when it came to the people she loved. I'd try to find more ways to be there for her in the coming months.

After all, it was only fair.

She had always been there for me, so it would be nice to be able to return the favor in any way that I could.

In the end, that was what being part of a family was all about.

Chapter 19

I HAD HALF-EXPECTED Lionel Henderson to make an appearance at the donut shop, but he never showed up. That just meant that Jake and I would have to track him down later. I wanted to ask both Lionel and Maxine about their money woes and the chances that they had access to a credible source of paper for counterfeiting. By using bills that were from the old design, they wouldn't have to use the fancy embedded plastic strips and watermarks, but they still had to be at least credible, and I had to imagine that would take a special supplier. How anyone would go about finding one was beyond me, but I knew Jake had access to resources that I couldn't even imagine. Until I finished up at the donut shop for the day, it would just have to wait, but I had some time to myself as my customers started tapering off, so I thought about all the facts we'd gathered so far.

Jake came in ten minutes before eleven, looking more than a little bored. "How's your morning been, Suzanne?"

"Better than yours, by the look of you," I said. "I'm sorry the flip house burned down."

"Not to mention Curtis Mason dying in the process. I've been going over it again and again in my head, and I have to believe that he saw something last night and got curious about it. Investigating it is what probably got him killed." Jake hesitated a moment before asking, "Suzanne, is it *my* fault he died in that fire last night?"

"What? Of course not," I said, doing my best to reassure him. "You can't think that for even a minute."

"Come on, you said something to that effect yesterday yourself when you tried to warn me about using him."

"Jake, you didn't *make* Curtis do anything. If he died because he was snooping around our project, that's on him, not you."

"I know you're probably right, but I still can't help feeling responsible about it. Have you heard from Chief Grant by any chance?"

I looked around at my three customers, all lingering over their coffee and staring at their phones. No one was paying any attention to us, but I still didn't want to go into too much detail, at least not where they could hear us talking. "Let me get you something to nibble on," I said.

"I'm good," Jake said, though I saw him staring longingly at the sour cream cake donuts.

"Go on, you burned off plenty of calories yesterday," I told him.

"I shouldn't," he said with some hesitation.

"Eat part of one, and then you can always throw the rest of it away," I told him as I wrapped a donut up in a napkin and handed it to him.

"Sure, like there's any chance of that happening," Jake said with a wry smile as he took his first bite.

"How about some coffee to go with it?"

"Sold," Jake said as he moved behind the counter to be closer to me. In a softer voice, he said, "Tell me what's happened so far."

In a brief recap, I brought him up to speed about my visits from Maxine and Momma and what we talked about. Jake nodded as I spoke and asked just enough questions to show that he was paying attention. "I have some ideas about how to track down that paper," he said after he polished off the donut in his hand.

"I keep thinking that I should have kept at least one of those bills," I told him.

"Suzanne, you don't want to be caught with counterfeit currency; trust me on that."

"I know what you're saying, but having some might help us track down the source," I told him.

"We'll just have to figure out a way to manage without it," my husband said. "How soon can you get out of here?"

I sighed heavily before I answered. "Unfortunately, I have a pile of dirty dishes, plates, cups, saucers, bowls, and utensils waiting for me," I said regretfully.

Jake looked around. "Where's Emma? I thought she was supposed to work today."

I didn't want to tell him what had happened, but I knew that it would come out sooner or later, so I realized that I might as well get it out of the way. "She was already here this morning when I showed up, but I sent her home."

He took that in, and then he said gently, "I'm sure you had your reasons."

"Jake, she let her father inside. He was sitting with her, and he wanted to grill me about the fire. I made him leave, and then I sent Emma home right after I threw him out."

Jake nodded. "I get that completely. You didn't have any choice."

"Are you sure I didn't overreact to the situation?" I'd been feeling bad about Emma's punishment all morning, and I really wanted Jake's take on the matter.

"The way I see it, you did the only thing you could do," Jake said as he put his mug down and patted my shoulder. "I'm proud of you. It's one thing to stand up to people you don't like, but you did it to one of your best friends. I doubt she'll make that mistake again."

"If she ever comes back at all, anyway," I said. "Barton has been after her for months to come work for him at the restaurant, and this might just be what sends her straight to him."

Jake shook his head. "She'll be back at Donut Hearts. I promise."

"Don't make promises you can't keep," I told him. I really was concerned about Emma leaving me for good, and saying it out loud to Jake somehow just made it more real.

"Okay, you're right. I can't promise you anything that I don't have control over, but I know how much she loves working here with you. Unless I badly miss my guess, she'll be back."

"I hope you're right," I said a bit sullenly.

"In the meantime, let me step in and help," my husband said. "I've done plenty of dishes in my life. Let me do them while you're working up here."

"I love you for making the offer, but you don't know where anything goes," I protested, using the same excuse I'd used with my mother. "I've already turned Momma down when she made me the exact same offer."

"The difference between her and me is that I'm not about to take no for an answer. Don't sweat it, you can fix whatever I mess up," Jake answered with a grin. "Come on. I won't even charge you for the labor."

"Unless we count the donut and the coffee you just had," I replied with a slight smile.

"Hey, those were going to be on the house anyway." He kissed the tip of my nose. "No more protests. I'm doing this."

"Okay. I appreciate it," I said.

He laughed at me. "The truth is that I thought you'd protest a bit more than that."

"What can I say? You made a persuasive argument, and those are a lot of dishes," I told him.

"I'm happy to do them." Jake headed back into the kitchen, and I suddenly felt better, though not because he was taking some of the work off my plate. Just having my husband nearby always buoyed my spirits.

We were a team, and I was so happy that I'd found him that I never took his presence in my life for granted.

Five minutes later, the police chief came by the shop. I was nearly ready to close anyway, and since no one was there at the moment, I flipped the sign to CLOSED and locked the door behind him. "Thanks for coming by, Chief."

"You're welcome. Do you happen to know where Jake is? I need to speak with him."

"He's in the kitchen, doing dishes," I said.

Chief Grant smiled at me. "Suzanne, if you don't want to tell me, don't, but you don't have to make up excuses. I'm a big boy, I can take it."

"Did I hear voices out here?" Jake asked as he came out of the kitchen wearing Emma's apron. It was clearly too small for him, but he managed to pull it off anyway. Backing up my earlier statement were soap bubble fragments still clinging to his hands and wrists as he wiped them with a towel. Jake had clearly used way too much soap, and I hoped that he'd at least rinsed everything properly, or I was going to have to do everything again. If I did, I'd never mention it to Jake, though. I didn't want anything to taint his kind offer.

"Were you really doing dishes?" the police chief asked my husband.

"It's really therapeutic," Jake answered. "You should try it yourself sometime. It gives you time to think about all kinds of things."

"Thanks, but I'll have to take your word for it. I'm more of a paper-plate kind of guy myself."

"Suit yourself," Jake said. "What's up?"

"I've been looking for you," the chief said.

"Hey, what about me? I'm part of this, too," I protested.

"You didn't let me finish," Chief Grant said. "I was going to ask Jake to join us here so I could tell you both what we found at the same time."

"I appreciate that," I said. "What's going on?"

The chief looked a little abashed. "It turns out that you were right after all, Suzanne. The autopsy was expedited by the Secret Service. Evidently Agent Blaze is back in town, making things happen."

"It doesn't surprise me one bit," I said. "What did they find?"

"Someone hit Curtis Mason in the back of the head with a shovel. The blade was uncovered in the fire, and it's a perfect match to the indent on the back of his skull."

"So he never even saw it coming," Jake said soberly.

"No, I don't think he did. There was also evidence that it happened outside. We found blood on the scene and what appeared to be scuff marks in the dirt where someone dragged him inside the house."

"That means that he was snooping, and he got caught red-handed," I said. "I'm sure Lionel Henderson is capable of doing it, and I don't doubt that Maxine Halliday could have done it, as well."

"What did she want when she was in here earlier?" the chief asked.

"You saw that?" I asked him.

"No, but I got a tip that you two were having some kind of argument in the donut shop around six o'clock this morning," the chief said. "What was she so upset about?"

"She threatened to sue me for telling you about her yesterday," I said, "but Momma talked her out of it. It might interest you to know that both Maxine and Lionel are in financial straits."

"I know that already," the chief said. "I'm surprised you found out so quickly, though." He paused a moment and turned to Jake. "Was that your doing?"

"No, Jake didn't tell me, Momma did," I interjected. "We're wondering where the counterfeiter found the paper they used to make those fake bills."

"Well, at least I can ease your mind on that score," the chief said. "We found the source."

"Really? Who was it?"

"I can't tell you that."

"Come on, Chief, we won't tell anyone," I protested.

"I can't tell you because I don't know. Agent Blaze made the arrest, and they are sweating the suspect for the name of their buyer even as we speak. I don't think it's going to do much good, though."

"Why not?" Jake asked. "Blaze is very good at what she does."

"Evidently the suspect has a long history of never even knowing the identity of whoever is paying for his services. He uses go-betweens exclusively, and if he should happen to know anything more than that, he keeps his mouth shut, no matter how much pressure is applied. Unless I miss my guess, it's going to be a dead end."

"Who's to say that the person under arrest isn't the counterfeiter, as well as being the killer?" I asked.

"It's doubtful. From what I was told, this guy is strictly a supplier, not an end user of what he traffics."

"Okay," I said. "That still leaves us with our main two suspects."

"You're not going after them again, are you?" the chief asked us. "That's really why I'm here. I've been told to officially discourage you both from looking into this any further."

"Did Blaze send you?" Jake asked softly.

"She happened to mention that if she caught anyone meddling in her case, they'd pay dearly for it. The funny thing is that I think she was talking about me as much as she was about the four of you. I'd leave this one alone if I were you, Jake." After a moment of contemplation, the chief added, "I don't have to tell you the woman's history. From what I've been able to find out, she never bluffs."

"I know that all too well myself," Jake said.

I looked at both men and scowled. "We're not just going to give up, are we?"

"Suzanne, you heard the man," Jake said. "We have to stay away from both of our suspects, or we're going to get ourselves into a jam that we can't get out of, even with my connections in law enforcement."

"Okay, I get that," I said, "but that doesn't mean we have to drop it altogether."

"What else is there for us to do?" Jake asked.

Instead of answering him directly, I turned back to the chief. "Do you still have the house cordoned off?"

"We're finished with our investigation there, if that's what you're asking, and so is the arson inspector. There was no doubt about the accelerants used, or the cause of murder, but Suzanne, there's nothing there to see. That place is too dangerous to walk around in."

"We won't go into the house itself, and besides, we'll be careful," I said.

"I'd strongly advise against it," the police chief said solemnly.

"Is that your official position or just one friend looking out for another?"

The chief looked more than a little bit frustrated. "You know that I can't keep you from going back. After all, you both are part owners of the property, but I can't protect you if Agent Blaze catches you there nosing around, either."

"I would never ask you to do that," I said. I saw him glance in the direction of one of the leftover boxes of donuts I was about to discard. "Would you mind doing me a favor?"

"If it's within my power, you know I will," he said.

"I'm just going to have to throw these out. Would you take them to the station and give them to your officers as my way of thanking them for a job well done?"

"I don't know if I should do that," the chief said. "You know I don't like to accept things of value that are free."

"These are all discards," I told him as I shoved the boxes into his hands. "If you don't take them off my hands, then I'll just have to chuck them into the dumpster. Don't make me do that. I hate to see good treats go to waste."

"Well, if it will help you out," he said with a quick grin, "I'm willing to pitch in and do my part."

"You're a real prince," I said with a grin as I held the door open for him.

After he was gone, I looked behind him, where I found Jake shucking his apron.

"What are you doing?" I asked him.

"Like you said, I'm heading to the building site," he said.

"Okay, I guess I'll meet you there when I'm finished here," I said as I started cleaning up the shop.

"You aren't coming with me?" Jake asked, clearly surprised.

"I'd love to, but I have work to do," I told him.

As he donned his apron again, he said, "I'll stick with it too, then."

"You don't have to, but if you're going to insist on going alone, you need to at least take Phillip with you."

"No, like I said, I'll wait for you." As he vanished back into the kitchen, he called out, "Just hurry, will you at least do that for me?"

"Chances are good that I'll be finished before you will be," I said.

"If that's a challenge, you're on," Jake answered.

"Take your time and do them right," I replied.

"You know me. I'm quick *and* efficient. What a lucky woman you are to have found me."

I returned his grin with one of my own. "You don't have to tell me that."

## Chapter 20

"YOU WANT THEM TO GO? Really?" Trish asked me as I ran into the Boxcar Grill to collect our burgers. Jake and I had decided to eat once we got to the house. I didn't account for Trish's reaction, though I should have anticipated that was how she would feel. "Suzanne, was it something I said or did? If it is, I'm truly sorry."

"Trish, it has nothing to do with you," I explained. "Jake and I just don't have a lot of time."

"Suzanne, it takes just as much time to eat in your Jeep as it does at one of my tables. Besides, the food isn't nearly as good if it's not served hot." I knew Trish didn't like take-out orders, but I'd never really tested her on it myself over the years.

"Would it make things right between us if Jake and I ate here?"

She pretended to be indifferent to my suggestion as she avoided my gaze. "I wouldn't want to hold you up."

I put my hands on her shoulders and made her look into my eyes. "I'll ask you again. Would it be okay if we ate here?"

"I'd love it," she said as she reached over and pulled out a chair at the table closest to her station up front by the register. "Look at that. I even saved you both seats."

"How could you do that?" I asked with a laugh. "You didn't even know we were coming."

"What can I say? I'm psychic."

"Did you say psychotic?" Charlie Granger asked as he held his bill out to her.

"Charlie, do you really want to pay my aggravation tax again?" Trish asked him coolly.

That quieted him down immediately. "No, ma'am. Sorry about that." He thrust a twenty at her as he fled the diner. "Keep the change."

After he was gone, I asked, "What was that all about?"

"It's something new I'm trying," Trish said as she processed his bill and put Charlie's change in the tip jar on the counter. "For egregious cases of offense, I charge a fifty percent surcharge on any bill at my sole discretion."

"Have you used it much?"

"So far I've only had to do it twice. It's amazing how quickly the word spreads," she said with a grin. "You should try it yourself at Donut Hearts."

"I don't think so. The truth is that I just couldn't bring myself to do it, not that I'm judging you," I said. "You just have more of a built-in clientele than I do."

"I get that. Anyway, it's actually more of a threat than an actual policy. Why don't you go get Jake, and I'll get Hilda started on your burgers. I'm guessing you want fries and tea with them, right?"

"That sounds perfect," I said.

I walked out to the truck, and Jake's smile faded into a frown when he saw that I was empty-handed. "What's going on?"

"Trish was offended when I asked for our food to go, so it turns out that we're eating inside. I hope that's okay with you."

Jake shrugged. "It's fine by me."

As we walked up the diner's steps together, I asked, "Are you sure that you're okay with this?"

"Suzanne, if it's important to Trish, it's easy enough to do. Say, have you heard about her latest thing?" he asked me with a grin.

"The aggravation tax? As a matter of fact, I just saw it in action."

"Was that why Charlie raced out so fast a minute ago?" Jake asked, laughing. "I can't believe it's true."

"She didn't actually enforce it," I explained. "The threat alone was enough to bring him into line."

"She's got some kind of a medieval fiefdom going on here, doesn't she?"

"I know I'd hate to offend her," I said, "and not just because she's one of my best friends in the world. Can you imagine life in April Springs without the Boxcar Grill?"

"No, it would truly be a sad and gloomy place," he said.

Trish smiled happily at both of us as we walked in, and not long after we took our seats, our food was served.

"Did you make this for someone else?" Jake asked as he looked at the burger and fries suddenly in front of him.

"No. I bumped your order to the head of the line. Being the owner has its privileges. Suzanne told me that you two were in a hurry."

"Thanks," Jake said as he took a bite. "This is amazing."

"I'm glad you approve," Trish said, and then she drifted off to wait on another customer. I didn't know how she managed to run the dining room, wait on customers, handle the register, *and* keep things hopping with Hilda in back. It would have driven me crazy in no time at all, but she did it with such grace and elegance that it was hard to imagine anyone else tackling it.

As we ate, Jake and I chatted idly with Trish, but we didn't dare speculate about the case, and our hostess was gracious enough not to ask us about it. The truth of the matter was that she might not even have known what had happened at the flip house yet. After all, not everyone in April Springs was up on what was going on outside the town limits.

Once our bill was paid, we were in Jake's truck and heading toward the house, or more accurately, what was left of it.

I wondered if it was even possible that we might find something that everyone else had missed. It was hard to imagine that between Chief Grant and his staff, the fire marshal, and the Secret Service, there would be anything left to find of value to the investigation, but we weren't about to let that stop us from trying.

If there was anything we could do to help catch the killer, we were bound and determined to do it.

As we drove past Curtis's place, Jake hesitated.

"What's up?" I asked him.

"Why isn't anybody here?" he asked. "The man was murdered yesterday. Don't you think that at least warrants a full-scale search of his place?"

"I'm sure somebody's checked it out," I said. "After all, they can't be everywhere at once."

"I suppose not," Jake said as he drove past.

As soon as we got near the flip house, I immediately understood why Curtis Mason's house was empty.

It appeared that everyone was at our burned-out place.

Chief Grant was driving out as we were heading in, and he stopped and motioned for us to roll down our windows so we could chat.

"What's going on?" Jake asked him.

"I was asked, ordered is more like it, to give Agent Blaze an update. That was easy enough, since I haven't made any real progress since we spoke last night, so it was short and sweet."

"What about Maxine and Lionel?" I asked.

"As of a few minutes ago, they're both unaccounted for," the chief said. "You can't even begin to imagine how frustrated the Secret Service is about that."

"They aren't blaming you, are they?" Jake asked him.

"Directly? No. But I can feel their scorn. I didn't realize it was my job to be everywhere at once."

"We were just saying the same thing," I told the chief, trying my best to comfort him.

"Well, she sent me out to find you, Suzanne, so at least that's something."

"Me? What does she want with me?"

The chief shook his head slightly. "She wants to hear all about your fight with Maxine this morning. Evidently you're the last person to see her today."

"There's nothing I can tell her that's going to help her find the real estate agent," I said.

"You know that, and I know that, but she's going to run you through the wringer anyway."

"Not without me, she's not," Jake answered.

"If anyone else made that claim, I'd have said they were delusional, but you might just have a fighting chance with her. Anyway, good luck." Almost as an afterthought, he said, "Sorry I ratted you out, Suzanne."

"No worries, Chief," I told him. "Did you tell her *everything* we discussed?"

"She's got it all," he admitted. "Like I said, I didn't have much of a choice."

"We understand," Jake said as he looked up. Agent Blaze was standing by her car watching us, and the moment she got our attention, she waved us toward her. "We'd better go."

"Good luck," the chief said, and then he was gone.

"I need to know everything you know," Agent Blaze said curtly. At first she'd tried to separate my husband and me, but she quickly realized that wasn't going to happen. That put her in a bad mood, not that she probably wasn't there anyway.

"I've already told you three times," I said wearily. "I don't know what else you expect me to say."

"There's got to be something you're missing," she insisted.

"Agent Blaze, my wife and I have cooperated with you fully, but there's simply nothing left for us to tell you."

"Fine. I'd like to know one more thing if I may."

"If we can help you, we will," I told her.

"Why are you both here right now?" She gestured to what remained of the house, mostly just charred rubble. "There's obviously nothing here worth saving."

"We wanted to see it again for ourselves," I said quickly. I wasn't about to admit that we were still digging into the counterfeiting ring and Curtis Mason's murder. "Is that okay with you?"

"It's fine. We were just leaving," she said. "Do you have any idea where either Maxine Halliday or Lionel Henderson III currently are?"

There was no doubt the question was an official one, and I was glad that I could give her an honest answer. "I don't have a clue," I said.

"Neither do I," Jake added.

"Then there's nothing keeping us here," she said as she gestured to her team, which was waiting patiently for some signal from their leader. As a unit, they got into the vehicles and started to drive away. Only Agent Blaze hesitated. "If you see either one of them or come across anything that might help the investigation, I expect you to report it directly to me, not your local chief of police. Do I make myself clear?"

"Crystal," Jake said, and I nodded my agreement as well.

She seemed satisfied by our responses, and soon enough, we were alone.

## Chapter 21

THE HOUSE WAS A TOTAL bust, and not just the fact that there was nothing left to remodel. If there was a clue in the burned-out rubble, we couldn't see it from the perimeter, and there was no way we were going to risk rooting around in what was left.

I was ready to give up when Jake asked, "Suzanne, where are you going?"

"Is there really any reason to hang around here anymore?"

"I thought we were looking for clues," Jake protested.

"In there? Even if there was anything there to find, don't you think between the three different investigating agencies they would have found it before us?"

"You've discovered things in the past when everyone else overlooked them," he reminded me.

"True, but not after a search like what happened here," I said, more than a little disheartened.

My husband put an arm around my shoulders. "Come on. Let's apply a little scientific method and see what we can find."

"What did you have in mind?" I was honestly curious about my husband's willingness to look over ground that had already been so thoroughly searched. "There's not much chance we'll find anything here," I said as I pointed to the ruins of what used to be our family project.

"So then we don't focus on there," he said.

"I'm willing to try anything at this point. I can't ever remember being so frustrated in an investigation when all seemed so lost," I admitted.

"That's why we need to take our emotions out of it. I know they usually serve you well, but let's look at this from a purely academic point of view. One of the first things they taught us at the academy were the different ways to search an area."

"What are they?"

"Grid is popular, and so are line and zone searches, but what I have in mind is a spiral pattern. We start from one corner of the burned-out house and circle it, expanding the area of our search as we go. What do you say?"

"It sounds as good as anything else to me. Go on. I'll follow you," I said.

"Actually, I was thinking that one of us should go clockwise and the other counterclockwise. It's possible that way we might see something from a different perspective."

"Okay, I'll go counterclockwise. After all, it seems to be in my nature to go against the grain," I said with a grin. "How far do we search?"

"Until we can't search anymore," Jake said.

I wasn't sure how long we'd be at it, but what else was there for us to do? Everybody was looking for Maxine and Lionel, so I doubted we could add anything to that part of the investigation, but maybe, just maybe, we'd get lucky here. If nothing else, it felt as though we were being productive. We stood back-to-back at one corner of the house and met up again on the opposite corner.

"Find anything yet?" I asked him with a grin.

"Suzanne, I didn't think we'd get immediate results," Jake answered.

"I was just kidding," I said as I extended my pattern a little farther out. I might not have been following Jake, but we met up twice in each circular pattern, so at least I got to see him briefly each time we passed. He was mostly just motion out of the corner of my field of vision, though. I was focused on the ground.

I found several things at my feet, mostly construction debris that had blown away from the house or the dumpster we'd used, but something caught my eye about forty feet from where the side door of the house used to be.

At first I thought I was imagining it. In fact, I almost passed it by when something in my head told me that it was worth investigating.

It had been covered by a leaf and part of a bit of torn drywall, but it was there nonetheless.

I had found Lionel Henderson's personal good luck token, the coin I'd seen him playing with several times before. I had to wonder when he'd lost it. It had certainly been *after* he'd claimed to have lost interest in buying our flip house.

I couldn't believe it, but I'd just found a genuine clue after all.

I'd knelt down to pick it up when Jake must have seen what I was up to and grabbed my arm. "Hang on. What did you find?"

"Unless I'm mistaken, I believe this is Lionel Henderson's lucky coin," I said.

"Hold on one second," Jake said as he pulled out his phone and started taking pictures of the nearly buried coin. Once he was satisfied that he had enough images, he took a pen from his pocket and carefully removed the debris around it, documenting it as he worked. It was a pleasure watching how meticulous he was at the job, and I could understand why he missed doing something with his life, particularly when he was clearly so good at what he'd once done for a living. Once the coin was fully exposed, he grabbed an evidence bag from his pocket and carefully collected it.

After that, he did something that surprised me.

He handed the bag to me.

"Are you certain this is Henderson's lucky token? I need you to be absolutely sure before I call Agent Blaze," Jake said.

I needed only a moment to confirm its identity. "It's the same one, all right, or a perfect duplicate of it," I said.

"Good. That's all I need to know."

Jake started to call the Secret Service agent when a voice called out from behind the small copse of trees that separated the burned-out house from Curtis Mason's former place.

"Stop what you're doing this instant," Lionel Henderson III said as he pointed a gun at Jake's heart. "I'll take that token, if you don't mind."

## Chapter 22

I HELD ONTO THE COIN, since it was our only bargaining chip. "Lionel, why did you use this house for your counterfeiting operation?" I asked him as Jake slowly started reaching for his gun, safely stashed away in his shoulder holster. To most people, it might have looked as though he was simply scratching his chest, but evidently the counterfeiter had been waiting for him to do something like it.

"You don't want to do that, Mr. Bishop. I may not be that great a shot, but surely I'll hit one of you if you continue to reach for that weapon. Do you really want to take that chance?"

"You don't want to kill us, Lionel," I said, hoping that it was true.

"At this point, I don't see why not. After all, I've already got the blood of two people on my hands. What's two more?"

"I understand that you killed Curtis Mason, but who else is dead?" I asked, hoping against hope that it wasn't one of my friends. What if Chief Grant had figured everything out and confronted him? Could this shadow of a man have murdered my friend?

Jake got it before I did, which was to be expected, given the fact that he was a seasoned detective. I was good, and I fully realized it, but it would be ridiculous of me to suspect that I was better than my husband. As a matter of fact, it was a point of pride with me.

"You killed Maxine Halliday," he said flatly.

"Very good, Detective. Now reach into your holster and slowly remove your handgun by your fingertips and drop it to the ground. Who knew that watching so many detective shows on television would give me insight into the way a law enforcement officer's mind worked?"

Jake glanced at me, and I just shrugged. It was his call, and I respected his judgment. If he thought he could get a shot off before Lionel could fire in our direction, then I was okay with the consequences of his actions, and I hoped he knew it.

I knew in my heart that sometimes a roll of the dice was the best you could do. You placed your bet, and you took your chances on the final outcome.

Jake pondered the decision for a moment before doing as he had been instructed. I'd been poised to dive to the ground if he'd decided to shoot, but I knew that we weren't out of options yet. I couldn't really blame my husband for not risking my life. I knew that if he had been alone, he would have taken his chances without a single moment of hesitation, but I was the mitigating factor here.

Maybe I could do something to distract the killer enough for Jake to come up with an alternate plan. "Why did you feel as though you had to kill Maxine?" I asked him.

"She thought she could blackmail me, if you can believe that," he said with disdain. "I was here collecting my supply of paper and some extra bills I'd already printed up when she followed me inside. I knew that she'd been snooping around the house, but I didn't see her at the time. I let my guard down for a moment, and that was all that it took."

"Why here, though?" I asked him again. "That's the part that I don't understand. You could have just as easily done this in your own home."

"And risk having someone discover what I was up to? I hardly think so. I knew this place had been virtually abandoned for quite some time, and it was perfect for my needs, or so I thought. That was before I realized just what a mistake I'd made in choosing this place."

"Why was everyone so interested in this property all of a sudden?" I asked. "After all, it was in pretty rough shape."

"You still don't get it, do you? It's not the house that's so valuable; it's the land it sits on," he said, shaking his head. "A new shopping center is going in on the abutting property, and this lot is going to be worth ten times what the house sold for."

"Why have I not heard about this until now? I can't imagine my mother not knowing about it," I said as I noticed that Jake was sizing things up. If we both dove at the same time, there was a chance he could retrieve his weapon and fire before Lionel could get off a clear shot at us. But he needed time to figure the angles and the risks, which meant that I had to stall more, which was okay with me, since I honestly wanted to know the answers to the questions I was asking.

"Contrary to what you might believe, your mother doesn't know *everything*," the killer said with a snort of derision. "This was hush-hush. As a matter of fact, I was surprised that Maxine knew about it. Anyway, she must have been over here and saw me go inside, so she followed me into the house."

"And you hit her?" I asked.

"What? No, of course not," he replied, acting offended by the very thought of striking a woman. This was one odd bird we were dealing with. He didn't mind killing two people, but he didn't want to be thought of as a woman beater. "She tripped on some construction debris and hit her head. I did my best to help her staunch the flow, but unfortunately, she spotted the bills I had been there to collect, and she figured it out. I should have done something about her then and there, but that was before I realized that I was going to have to do a few rather distasteful things if I was going to get out of this in one piece."

"Why kill Curtis, though?" I asked. "Did you catch him snooping, too?"

"The fool wouldn't leave well enough alone and mind his own business," Lionel said with distaste. "I had no choice."

"So you killed him and set fire to the house to hide the murder," Jake said.

"Yes, it seemed like a good idea at the time. However, Maxine figured out what I'd done, and she decided to blackmail me, not only for the counterfeiting but for the murder as well. She demanded half of everything I'd made up to that point, but I needed all of it if I was going to be able to get myself out of the financial pinch I was in. I'd done all of the work, and at that point I'd taken all of the risks, so there was no way I was going to split the proceeds with her. Besides, I knew that if I gave in to her the first time, she'd bleed me until I was dry. I couldn't let her get away with that, now could I?"

"Where's her body?" I asked as Jake motioned me downward with his gaze. I knew he was getting ready to act.

"They'll find her in her car by the lake with a typed suicide note confessing everything, including the arson and murder. To make matters more convincing, there will be paper and counterfeit bills in her trunk. As a matter of fact, I'm surprised they haven't found her yet."

"Give them time," I said. "It was careless of you to drop your good-luck token here," I said, trying to goad him a little. If he were upset, maybe it would interfere with his aim. At least that was my hope. "Either that, or you were just stupid."

I glanced at Jake and saw him smile briefly. At least I had his approval.

It worked as planned. Lionel's face grew red. "That witch stole it from me without me noticing and planted it here! It was her way of ensuring that I didn't double-cross her."

"And she just told you that of her own free will?" I asked. Jake had left all the questioning to me, and I had a hunch I knew why. Lionel was focusing solely on me, which was what my husband wanted. It might buy him a split second more time, which, knowing my husband, might be all that he needed.

"I had to use a little persuasion on her," he admitted, looking a bit disgusted by the memory of what he must have had to do to garner a confession out of her. "I didn't enjoy it, but it had to be done." He looked around the clearing to be sure we weren't being watched, which was the opportunity Jake had clearly been waiting for.

"Down!" he shouted at me, and I threw the coin at Lionel before hitting the dirt as hard and as fast as I could.

Lionel spun around as Jake dove for his weapon, but he was a split second too late.

In what felt like slow motion to me, Jake grabbed his handgun from the ground and seemed to fire the second his fingers wrapped around the handle.

Lionel Henderson III looked puzzled as the bullet hit him squarely in the chest and he was shoved backwards by the blow.

He hadn't even had time to get off a single shot, and it appeared that he was dead before his body even hit the ground.

## Chapter 23

JAKE RUSHED OVER TO me before he even checked the body, whether he was too worried about me or because he was so sure of his shot I couldn't say. "Suzanne, are you okay?"

As he helped me stand, I said, "Thanks to you, I didn't get a scratch on me. That was some shooting."

"It was all automatic," Jake said as we walked over to Lionel's body together. Just for good measure, Jake knelt down and pulled the gun out of the dead man's fingers, but it was clear that Lionel Henderson III hadn't stood a chance.

"Are you all right?" I asked him. I couldn't imagine it was ever easy killing someone, even if it was in self-defense, and I remembered when I had had to do it once. I had been shaken for a very long time from the experience, and I still had nightmares about it occasionally.

"I'm fine," he said, though there was a hard edge to his voice as he spoke. "When it came down to it, it was either him or us, and I'll choose us, ten out of ten."

"Thank you for saving me," I said as I stroked his arm lightly.

"I couldn't have done it without you," he replied.

"I kind of doubt that."

"Suzanne, he was so involved in answering your questions I knew that all I had to do was wait for him to be distracted and act. You were perfect."

In the distance, we heard police sirens. Someone must have heard the shot and reported it. The truth was that I was still so shaken by what had just happened that I had completely forgotten to call the police.

"Right back at you," I said as we waited for the authorities to arrive.

## Chapter 24

TWO WEEKS LATER, JAKE and I were enjoying a quiet evening at home. Momma had just called with news, and I couldn't wait to share it with my husband. "We are going to make an unbelievable profit on the flip house after all. Momma just sold the land to the developer, and she got a pretty penny for it."

"That's nice," Jake said absently.

"Aren't you pleased? After all, it was because of your push that we bought the place."

"Suzanne, I wanted a project, not an instant profit. It was the work I was interested in, not how much we could earn from it," he explained.

I curled up on the couch beside him. "I know that, but this all could have turned out a great deal worse than it did. I thought you'd be pleased. We managed to do quite a lot in a short span of time."

"And three people are dead because of it," Jake said a bit morosely.

"*None* of that was our fault, and you know it," I scolded him. "Lionel was the catalyst to everything bad that happened, and if we hadn't stopped him, he would have literally gotten away with murder."

"I know all of that, but it still leaves me a little dead inside," Jake said. "Suzanne, what am I going to do with the rest of my life?"

I thought about responding that he could just keep on loving me, but I knew that wasn't the real question he was asking me. "I honestly wish I knew," I said.

"So do I," Jake answered, and then he put his arm around me. "Anyway, we don't have to figure it out tonight, or even this week, but sometime, and I mean sometime soon, I've got to come up with a plan."

"You will," I said. "I have faith in you."

"Don't think for one second that I'm not thankful for that fact every single day of my life," Jake replied. It was clear he wanted to shake the somber mood he was in. "Do you feel like pie? There's still enough in the fridge to split from the apple crumb your mother brought over this afternoon."

"Well, we'll just have to remedy that, won't we?" I asked him as I started to get up.

"Stay right there. I'll serve you," Jake said with a smile as he got up and went into the kitchen.

As I waited for him to return, I thought about everything we'd been through lately. This entire adventure had begun because my husband had needed a purpose in life, which I completely understood, and I was going to do everything in my power to help him find it. In the meantime, Phillip's MRI was scheduled for the next day, so we'd have a better idea of what we were dealing with as far as his health issues were concerned. If we were lucky, the scan would show the cancer was still just in his prostate, something that could be remedied with surgery. If it were more widespread, we'd find a way to deal with that, too.

After all, we were family, and in the end, that was really all any of us ever had, whether we were related by blood, by marriage, or simply by love.

# Baked Chocolaty Donuts

I love chocolate, as anyone who knows me can testify. Donuts seem to me to be an excellent delivery device when I need something in particular. I've made chocolate donuts using cake mixes and even doctored brownie mixes, and while they've all been good, this one is a real winner. Give it a try when your sweet tooth is craving something warm and chocolaty.

Ingredients

1 cup unbleached all-purpose flour

1/2 cup unsweetened cocoa powder

1 teaspoon baking powder

1/2 teaspoon baking soda

1/2 teaspoon nutmeg

1/2 teaspoon cinnamon

1/8 teaspoon of salt

1 egg, beaten

1/2 cup whole chocolate milk

4 tablespoons salted butter, melted

1/2 cup granulated sugar

1 1/2 teaspoons vanilla extract

Directions

Preheat your oven to 350°F.

While you are waiting for your oven to reach temperature, take a medium-sized bowl and combine the flour, cocoa, baking powder, baking soda, nutmeg, cinnamon, and salt and sift together.

In another, somewhat larger bowl, beat the egg and then add the chocolate milk, butter, sugar, and vanilla extract.

Slowly add the wet mix to the dry mix, stirring until it's incorporated, but being careful not to overmix.

Add the batter to cupcake pans or donut molds and bake for 10 to 15 minutes, or until an inserted toothpick comes out clean.

Once the donuts are done, remove them to a cooling rack.

These donuts can be topped with chocolate icing, a simple chocolate glaze, or chocolate sprinkles or eaten plain.

Makes 6 to 9 donuts, depending on your pan size.

# A Classic Fried Donut

This is my go-to recipe when I'm craving a simple donut that's easy to make and still satisfies my hungry horde. It can be tweaked in a variety of ways, but when all else fails you, this one shouldn't let you down.

Ingredients

7 cups unbleached all-purpose flour

2 teaspoons baking soda

2 teaspoons nutmeg

2 teaspoons cinnamon

3 dashes of salt

2 eggs, beaten

2 cups granulated sugar

1 cup sour cream

2 cups milk

Enough canola or peanut oil for frying your donuts

Directions

Heat your oil to 375°F. While you're waiting for it to come up to temperature, in a medium-sized bowl, sift together the flour, baking soda, nutmeg, cinnamon, and salt.

In a larger bowl, beat the eggs and then add the sugar, sour cream, and milk, stirring until combined. Slowly add the dry ingredients to the wet, mixing until you get everything incorporated. More milk or flour can be used to achieve the texture you're looking for.

Knead the dough lightly, then roll it out to 1/4-inch thickness. Using your donut cutter, cut the donut shapes, reserving the holes for a later frying.

Add four donuts to the oil at a time, being careful not to overcrowd the pot.

Cook for 2 minutes on each side, flipping halfway.

Remove to a wire rack to drain under paper towels, and then dust with powdered sugar or make a simple glaze with confectioners' sugar, vanilla extract, and milk until you reach the desired consistency.

Makes 6 to 8 donuts and corresponding holes, depending on your cutter size.

# Pineapple Upside-Down Donuts

Since Momma makes a pineapple upside-down cake in the book, I thought I'd add one of my variations as well. While it's not truly a cake, with the pineapple pieces and the maraschino cherries, it's the next best thing!

Ingredients

1 can crushed pineapple (8.5 oz.)

12 maraschino cherries, cut in quarters

1 egg, beaten

2 1/2 tablespoons granulated sugar

1 cup all-purpose flour

1/2 teaspoon baking soda

1/2 teaspoon baking powder

Dash of salt

1/4 teaspoon nutmeg

Directions

Heat enough canola oil to 375°F to fry your donuts.

While you're waiting for it to come to temperature, empty the entire can of crushed pineapple, juice and all, into a large bowl. Next, add the diced maraschino cherries, beaten egg, and sugar, and stir until blended.

In a separate bowl, sift together the flour, baking soda, baking powder, salt, and nutmeg.

Then gently add the dry ingredients to the wet, stirring enough to mix nicely until the batter is smooth.

When the oil comes up to temperature, drop a tablespoon of batter into the hot oil and repeat the process, being careful not to overcrowd the pot. This step can be dangerous, so be careful!

After 2 minutes, check for doneness and then flip the donut drops, frying for another minute on the other side.

Drain on a wire rack with paper towels under it to catch the excess oil, dust with powdered sugar, and enjoy!

Makes approximately 8 to 12 small donuts.

If you enjoy Jessica Beck Mysteries and you would like to be notified when the next book is being released, please visit our website at jessicabeckmysteries.net for valuable information about Jessica's books, and sign up for her new-releases-only mail blast.

Your email address will not be shared, sold, bartered, traded, broadcast, or disclosed in any way. There will be no spam from us, just a friendly reminder when the latest book is being released, and of course, you can drop out at any time.

Other Books by Jessica Beck

Tasty Trials
Baked Books
Cranberry Crimes
Boston Cream Bribes
Cherry Filled Charges
Scary Sweets
Cocoa Crush
Pastry Penalties
Apple Stuffed Alibies
Perjury Proof
Caramel Canvas
Dark Drizzles
Counterfeit Confections
The Classic Diner Mysteries
A Chili Death
A Deadly Beef
A Killer Cake
A Baked Ham
A Bad Egg
A Real Pickle
A Burned Biscuit
The Ghost Cat Cozy Mysteries
Ghost Cat: Midnight Paws
Ghost Cat 2: Bid for Midnight
The Cast Iron Cooking Mysteries
Cast Iron Will
Cast Iron Conviction
Cast Iron Alibi
Cast Iron Motive
Cast Iron Suspicion

Made in the USA
Lexington, KY
15 May 2019